STORIES RULE PRESS PRESENTS

I0562886

Space Opera Digest
2021
FIGHT OR FLIGHT

Edited by Mark Posey

• Cameron Cooper • Benjamin Cooper • David A. Gray •
• Blaze Ward • Clayton Scott • Eliot Bishop •

STORIES RULE
EDMONTON • ALBERTA

FIRST EDITION: January 2021

Mark Posey (Ed.)
Bishop, Eliot
Cooper, Cameron
Cooper, Benjamin
Gray, David A.
Scott, Clayton
Ward, Blaze

Science Fiction—Fiction
Space Opera—Fiction

IngramSpark ISBN: ###
Amazon KDP Print ISBN: ###

About Fight Or Flight

What does one do in the face of a relentless enemy?

Stories Rule Press presents: Space Opera Digest 2021: Fight or Flight.

Fight or flight is one of our most primal instincts, a leftover from primitive days. It cannot be denied. In the backwater colonies on the fringes of outer space, it is one of our most valuable skills.

Ptolemy Lane. Sergeant Fisher. The Dagger. Senior Chief Jack Palahniuk. Jedidiah Kramer. Captain Hedge. Six heroes face that choice.

Fight or flight.

"The Captain Who Broke the Rules" by Cameron Cooper
"Stranded" by Benjamin Cooper
"Dagger" by David A. Gray
"Plankholder" by Blaze Ward
"The Sentry" by Clayton Scott
"Talionis" by Eliot Bishop

Six stories. Six relentless enemies and six epic heroes. What will they do? How will they survive?

Space Opera Digest 2021: Fight or Flight is the first volume in a quarterly collection of genre fiction anthologies presented by Stories Rule Press.

Space Opera Science Fiction Anthology

Foreword

Mark Posey

Stories Rule Press was formed out of the global pandemic of 2020. It had always been my wife's and my plan to get our writing income to the point where it could support us without the need of the dreaded day job. She had been writing full time for five years and when the layoffs and the lockdowns and the severance pay came in March of 2020, we just decided to go for it.

It was a huge adjustment at first, especially in mindset. I remember conversations where we both had to remind ourselves, "This is our job now. This is what we do." It's taken a long time. As I write this in early January of 2021, I think we've finally got it all worked out.

One of the things that is key for me in any work that I do is helping others. I knew very early on during the planning of the Stories Rule Press agenda that I would be editing a series of anthologies. Although I don't claim to be able to make someone's career, I do hope that, in some small measure, I can have a hand in their success.

Space Opera Digest 2021 is the first of what I hope are many anthologies from Stories Rule Press. It's been an interesting experience putting it together. Again, it's all about mindset. A lot of the time, I've felt like I was guessing at what needed to be done. I've had to trust that whatever choices I made were in the best interest of not only Stories Rule Press but the authors, as well. In the end, I think we've come up with a damn good set of stories from some exceptional writers. I'm proud to put them together under the Stories Rule Press name for your enjoyment and entertainment.

The only guidance I gave authors for a submission to the anthology was that it had to be space opera and a relentless enemy. I wanted them to feel as free as possible to be creative and come up with their best possible story. I've picked the six best out of all the stories submitted.

Here, for the first time, Stories Rule Press presents *Space Opera Digest 2021: Fight or Flight.*

Enjoy

Mark Posey
January 2021

The Captain Who Broke The Rules: A Ptolemy Lane Tale

Cameron Cooper

I've known Cameron Cooper for a long time. He's one of the inaugural authors at Stories Rule Press and I just love his work. His Imperial Hammer series has been a spectacular success as has The Indigo Reports. He's in the process of plotting the sequel to the Imperial Hammer series as this volume comes out and I'm very much looking forward to digging into those later in the year. I'd also very much like to see a series based around the Ptolemy Lane character from this story.

If you enjoy this story, you can find out more about Cameron's work at **https://CameronCooperAuthor.com.**

Enjoy "The Captain Who Broke the Rules". — MP

————————

On my third day aboard the *Jan Mayen Island*, I woke to find a memo from Captain Sandor waiting for me to accept delivery.

This is to inform you that at 02.47.45 hours this morning, ship's time, the following cargo containers with serial numbers registered to your passenger profile were jettisoned.

JMI-1340-9850-AOU0892-GTX

JMI-1340-9850-AOU0893-GTX

JMI-1340-9850-AOU0894-GTX

As a state of emergency was in force at the time, no warranties can be claimed.

Thank you and enjoy the rest of your journey aboard the Jan Mayen Island.

Cptn. D. Sandor

I skipped breakfast. I couldn't have eaten it, anyway. Instead, I headed for the Courtyard, where the thirty or so passengers on the *JMI* tended to spend their waking hours, to get away from the cramped quarters. At least you could stretch out your legs in the Courtyard.

I wasn't there to stretch my legs, though. Not today. My intention was to find out why my cargo had been dumped, and what I could do about it. There was always a senior crew member on hand in the Courtyard. They rotated through concierge duty one after the other, and no one but the Captain herself was exempt.

Thirty seconds in the Courtyard told me mine was not an isolated case. *Everyone* was bunched around the poor sod of an officer who'd snagged this shift, their voices lifted in protested, demanding their possessions back.

"That was everything I own!"

"We've moving to Bryant. How the hell are we supposed to survive on Bryant with *nothing*? It's a class three settlement!"

"It took me ninety years to build that collection!"

The officer was a slip of a girl, with a smart board and patience that was wearing thin. I lingered long enough to hear her start to repeat herself, then turned and scanned the Courtyard. The crew common room was on the other side of the Courtyard, through a wide doorway.

I headed over there and was halted at the opening by a sergeant who was only a bit bigger than the girl trying to placate the other passengers, but not as big as me.

He didn't seem to be bothered by the weight and height differences. "Sorry, this area is for crew only." He didn't move a centimeter, not even when I got up close.

"That's right. I'm looking for the Captain." I peered over his shoulder and around the common room. It had smaller tables and chairs, the same food printers that were in the Courtyard, and off-duty crew gobbling down breakfast.

Among them I spotted the Captain's cap of black hair, half-a-head higher than anyone else at her table. "Captain!" I shouted.

She paid no attention. The others at the table were heads-together with her, talking softly.

"Hey, buster, back off!" the sergeant said, gripping my arm. "She don't need passengers in her face this morning."

"I'm not in her face," I pointed out. "I'm right here." I filled my lungs and bellowed, "*Sandor!*"

This time, she looked up. The blue eyes narrowed.

The sergeant shook me like a wet rag. This was the reason he was on door duty this morning. They were expecting something like this.

I let him shake and held his gaze.

He stopped but didn't let go of my arm.

"You think I couldn't get through you if I wanted?" I asked him. "I'm being polite, but frankly, that's the most you should expect. I want answers. You jettisoned my freight and it was important to me."

"Everyone's freight was important." He shrugged.

"Not like mine was."

"I've got this, Finlay," Captain Sandor said, from behind the Sergeant.

I peered around him once more. "Hello Captain."

She stood close by the nearest table, her arms crossed. "Step around," she told me. "You get sixty seconds."

Finlay sighed and waved me through with a disgusted look.

I stepped around, moved over in front of her.

"I gotta hand it to you, Lane," she told me. "Three days is all it took for you to forget what I said when you came aboard."

"I haven't forgotten what you said," I assured her. "You made an impression."

The day I'd boarded, I had barely got my duffel stowed in the tiny stateroom when the door announced the Captain was outside, then slid aside to let her in.

She stood just inside the door—which put us barely a meter apart—and crossed her arms as she was now. She had long legs and thrust one of them to the side and measured me. "So you're Ptolemy Lane."

I hid my sigh. Lots of people had heard of me, but so far on this trip I'd managed to avoid anyone getting in my face with rumors they'd heard about me, or stories they'd been told that they objected to. "The fringes are getting way too small," I muttered. "You are...?"

"Sandor," she said shortly. "Here's the thing, Lane. You're used to running your town—"

"It's Georgina's Town, not my town," I corrected her. "And I'm really not the man who runs it."

"You kick people out. You get to decide who stays and who goes." Her tone was withering. She stepped a little closer. "You don't get to decide anything while you're on my ship. Is that clear?" The single overhead light gleamed in the pitch black of her hair, which was sable smooth, trimmed into a flat cap that accentuated her cheekbones...although I had the feeling she'd cut it to keep it out of the way, and couldn't give a damn about displaying her cheeks,

10

which were thinned and tight with anger right now.

I raised a brow. "Crystal clear," I said.

"I don't like trouble," she added. "I just want to get my passengers to Abbatangelo."

"That's all I'm looking to do," I told her truthfully. "What *have* you heard about me, Captain, to make you feel you have to warn me?"

"I've heard enough." She considered me once more. "You are too used to controlling things for yourself. People like you cause problems on a small ship like the *Jan Mayen*. I'm heading those problems off right now. Behave yourself, Mr. Lane."

She backed up and raised a hand at the door control. The door opened. She looked at me once more, expectantly.

"I'll behave myself," I had told her.

She'd turned and left without another word. And for three days, I *had* behaved myself as promised. Tossing my cargo broke that agreement, though.

I faced Sandor now and said, "What was the state of emergency?"

"What?"

"The emergency that made you jettison cargo...*all* the cargo, I'm starting to think." The voices in the Courtyard were getting louder as more people came to find out why their baggage was gone.

"There is no emergency," she said with a soothing tone.

"Then you lied about the emergency status to avoid the claims? That makes ejecting the freight even less understandable."

Her mouth opened. Her eyes narrowed. Then she sank onto the table behind her and stretched out her legs. "There is no emergency," she repeated. "But there was."

"And now there isn't, because you tossed..." I caught my breath

11

as everything clicked into place. "For the *speed*," I breathed. "You blew the freight to get better speed."

The blue eyes were cold. "You know a little about space flight, then." She sighed. "Enough to be hazardous." She glanced around, looking for eavesdroppers, which was interesting, given we were in the crew section, among people she was supposed to trust. "I will tell you, Mr. Lane, because I know you will badger me until you get answers that satisfy you. But you cannot share this with anyone. Panic, in a small ship, is contagious. Panicked passengers are dangerous."

Keeping the passengers ignorant was a backhanded way of protecting them. But she had correctly guessed that I would prod and insist until she told me what was going on. So maybe she was right about that, too. "What was the emergency?"

She hesitated, then said. "There was a slaver ship on our tail."

I drew in a deep, slow breath, riding out my reaction, my thoughts racing. Sandor didn't really have to say much else. I could figure it all out from there. The fringes were full of murderers, thieves, pirates and con artists of every stripe. Slavers put all of them to shame. They were the moldy edges of the underbelly of Terran territories. They attacked ships out in space, where the ship was cut off and vulnerable. They would plant a reactor-killer in the engine room while the ship was still in dock, then following them through space until the killer fired, bringing the ship to a body-smearing halt. They would board, scrape the ship of anyone still alive, and take them back to the pleasure domes in the Galxinayah quadrant.

Of the thousands of people taken by slavers, only a half dozen had ever escaped the domes. Those six survivors had revealed the truth about slavery in the domes, which went well beyond sex service. Experimental surgery. Mutilations, gladiator fights, target practice, hunting safaris. Whatever a customer wanted and could afford, they got, no matter how sick or perverted.

It was unusual for slaver ships to operate in this quadrant, although they obeyed no rules but their own. Maybe they were sizing up the neighborhood, preparing to move onto virgin territories ripe with new slaves.

A slaver ship on our asses could only mean that this ship had been targeted. And Sandor had dumped the cargo to increase her speed.

Interstellar flight was dictated by a ruthless equation involving the limits of speed, mass, inertia and the amount of energy the ship could carry with it. You could have more of one if you gave up one of the others, but you couldn't have all of them. Neither could you veer outside the lane to your destination because that would use up fuel you didn't have and guarantee you didn't make it.

Sandor had given up mass, to gain speed. As she considered the emergency over, she had gained enough speed to pull away from the slaver, which was bound by the same immoveable laws.

"You found the reactor-killer, then," I said.

Sandor frowned. "We will." She got to her feet. "Your sixty seconds are up, Mr. Lane. Please return to the passenger section of the ship."

"You're breaking the rules."

She tilted her head. "Rules?"

I nodded. "Didn't they tell you it would be smarter to stand down, let them board and take their pick of the passengers, and preserve your ship and crew?"

Her face worked. Anger glittered in her eyes. "No captain would ever—"

"They all do," I assured her. "They tell good tales about surviving by the skin of their teeth. They all lie, and the owners of their ships pat them on the head for it. But you're not doing that. Why is that?"

Her jaw worked. "None of your business. Good day, Mr. Lane."

The next bit of the puzzle dropped into place in my mind with a nearly audible click. "You have a history with them..." I breathed.

Sandor sank back down onto the edge of the table. The blue of her eyes was stormy. With another quick check around for observers, she reached up and pulled aside the open neck of her uniform tunic, to reveal the flesh over her heart. It was scarred with jagged pink ridges, radiating out from a white divot that was nearly circular.

"A governor," I said and swallowed. The governors were devices implanted over the heart and attached to the nervous system. It made the dome slaves compliant and delivered pain when they weren't. The only way to remove a governor without a fully equipped surgery was to tear them out, roots and all, then thrust white hot metal against the wound to cauterize it before you bled out.

It left a distinct scar like the one Sandor had on her chest.

"You're one of the six," I said.

"Is that what I am?" She let the tunic drop back over the scar.

"How long were you in the domes?"

"Long enough." She put her hands together, an oddly peaceful gesture. "Twenty-three years. Then I got lucky."

I wondered how much luck was involved. Twenty-three years was longer than most survived the domes. She had a powerful will to survive. It gave her the ruthlessness necessary to blow a ship full of passenger cargo and probably her paying freight, too.

14

"So you see, I won't stand by and let them take their pick," she added, her tone conversational. But there was a glitter in her eyes that belied the tone. "And I don't give a damn what you think, Mr. Lane."

"You don't like me." I only now recognized the distaste making her mouth curl.

"It's nothing personal."

"I think it is," I countered. "I've never met you, but you have already decided you don't like me. I don't think it is just my reputation for stirring up trouble."

"You have far too much personal power, Mr. Lane, which I think is dangerous in the fringes. Too much power in one set of hands leads to misery."

"Depends on who is holding it."

"Not really." Her tone was very cool. "Not long after I got this—" and her hand touched the tunic over the scar, "I applied for a resident ticket in Georgina's Town. Everyone says it is peaceful there. That you don't have to look over your shoulder all the time." She shrugged.

Now I got it. "You were turned down."

Her eyes were cold as she stared at me.

"Who gets to live in Georgina's Town…that's not my decision. I don't even get a say in it. I'm paid to keep the peace among the folks who live there, that's all."

"I think you're selling yourself short, Mr. Lane. I think you have far more power than you claim."

"Let me help you find the reactor-killer," I countered.

"Why? To demonstrate you're a nice guy?" Her tone conveyed how inadequate such a gesture would be.

I didn't get to answer her because a no-striper came running up, sweat making his temples glisten and staining the shirt under his arms. "Captain! Sir! Captain…"

He was shaking, his eyes wide as he stared at the captain. I don't think he even noticed me standing there.

"What is it, Jardine?" Sandor got to her feet. She was tall, but not skinny.

"Sir, it's Sahak! He's…" Jardine swallowed and leaned toward her, his face pale. "He's been eaten!" he mumbled.

*

I KEPT MY MOUTH SHUT and followed the pair of them through the ship, down into the crew-only levels where the corridors were dimmer, narrower and not at all straight. We bent around piping, ducked under housing, and dropped down steep stairs, and up more of them. I think Sandor forgot I was with them.

The ashen-faced crew we passed were too shocked to react when they spotted me. I was wearing clothes dark enough to be taken as a crew uniform at first glance and they looked like their thoughts were anywhere but the here and now.

Someone had pulled themselves together enough to rig temporary lighting, shining upon a spot deep behind hulking machinery making soft noises. The floor here was oil-stained and scuffed. We ducked under low pipes and straightened up, the temporary light sending our shadows playing over the bulkhead in front of us.

I noticed the slight concave curve of the wall and realized that I was staring at the inner lining of the exterior fuselage.

An officer with three stripes on his sleeve, the only three-stripe I had seen, put himself in front of Sandor. "It's bad, captain," he said, his tone gentle.

"Jardine said he'd been eaten, Mr. Harel. Was he lying?"

Harel swallowed. "No, sir."

Sandor waved him aside.

He moved, giving her a clear view. She examined the body. Harel was in my way, so all I could see was a pair of all-grip soles. I didn't think it would be smart to demand the XO move so I could see, so I kept my mouth zipped.

There was blood on one of the soles. Sahak had still been alive and on his feet while he was bleeding enough to form puddles. Poor bastard.

Sandor's jaw rippled, while she held her face immobile. "How long, Jones?" she asked.

Jones was hidden by Harel's body. She sounded as though she was standing right over Sahak when she said, "Maybe twelve hours, captain. It's hard to tell because there's…so little left. No kidneys, which are the best indicators."

Sandor nodded. "Give the body respect," she told Harel. Her mouth turned down. "We have more than enough space in the holds to let him ride home with us."

"There's more, Captain," Harel said, and hesitated.

She just raised one curved brow.

"I've got two more crew missing," Harel said.

Sandor took that one with the same calm. She nodded. "Everyone on search detail, Mr. Harel. In pairs. Issue weapons — handguns for now, all low voltage."

Low voltage would save a bolt from searing through the outer fuselage, but it limited the firepower of the guns, too. Everything is a trade-off in space.

Harel lifted a hand and clicked his fingers. Instantly, the crew standing around all shifted and moved. I heard shouting behind us, as the order was relayed.

A no striper dipped and wove his way up to us, carrying a half-empty sack. He held the sack out to the captain and the XO. They dug into the sack one after another and extracted a handgun each.

Around us, the crew had dispersed silently. They had gone to search for the missing crew, as ordered. That left me and Sandor, Harel and the no-striper, who took out the last handgun in the sack and tossed the sack away.

Sandor pointed at Harel and the no-striper. "You two, that way."

Harel waved at the no-striper, who moved back up the crooked alley to the main corridor. Harel followed and for the first time, I saw the body. I wished I hadn't. I rubbed at my mouth and looked away.

Sandor was watching me.

I lowered my hand. "You can't search alone."

"No." She waved me ahead. "That way."

Past the body.

I glanced at the remains as I carefully stepped past. My hand twitched. I wanted a widowmaker to grip but wasn't stupid enough to ask for one. Sandor would boot me back up to the passenger levels if I did.

As soon as the space widened, Sandor stepped up alongside me, then took point, two paces ahead. I listened for anything behind us, or to either side. It was cramped down here. Space was at a premium and pathways for mere people was a secondary consideration.

We hadn't searched for long when we found the vomit.

The steaming, knee-high pile sat on the floor in the middle of the by-way, cutting off our route. The stench was hot, scraping at the back of my throat and making my guts cramp.

I remembered the smell, now I was inhaling it once more, which made me very unhappy. "Let me see," I told Sandor. I made myself move up to the pile and bend over it. "It's too dark here," I said. "But the smell..."

"It's unmistakable," Sandor said quietly.

I looked at her. In the dark, all I could see was the hollow plane of one cheek and a dark eye pit. "A septimal," I concluded.

Septimals were ferocious carnivores that semi-digested their meals, regurgitated them, and came back to consume the vomit once the stomach acids had finished the job. They were a thigh high mass of muscle, teeth, jaws, six legs, two beady main eyes and two peripheral eyes, and a dark brown, glistening carapace that could withstand just about anything fired or thrown at it.

"How did one get on the ship?" I breathed. They were native to a barren ball deep inside slaver territory.

Sandor didn't linger to wonder with me. She moved carefully around the pile and over to the wall. There was a concierge panel there. She prodded it. "Harel! Respond!"

As she waited for the XO to hear she was calling for him and make his way to the nearest panel, she looked at me. "Septimals key in on pheromones. They pick a flavor they like and hunt it down. Nothing stops them but hard vacuum."

"High voltage guns slow them down."

"Vacuum is surer."

"Harel here, Captain," Harel's voice announced from the panel.

"Issue the widowmakers, Mr. Harel. Everyone in fours, now, watching all four directions."

"Captain?"

"There's a septimal onboard."

"A what?"

I winced.

Sandor rode right over her XO's ignorance. To be fair, most people hadn't heard of septimals. They were rarely seen in Terran territory. She told Harel, "You can't kill the thing that took Sahak. You can herd it with the widowmakers, though. Push it toward the airlock at the back of hold three. And stay out of its way if it takes a run at you."

"Jump up," I interjected.

"Climb out of its way," Sandor told Harel. "It will leave you alone if you're not the right sort of pheromones."

"I...ah...okay. Right, Captain." I could hear Harel pull himself together.

Sandor switched off, then bent and pressed her fingers against the panel beneath the communications board.

It swung open. A pilot light inside showed a rack of two-handed widowmakers. She reached in and took one, checked the charge, switched it on, then tossed it to me. I just barely got my hands up in time to catch it.

She bent and took out a second gun and shut the locker. The locks thunked back into place. She looked me. "You're a law maker, aren't you? Help me keep the peace on my ship."

"Very well." I checked the charge and the ready switch myself and tucked it under my arm. "Which way is hold three?"

She pointed. "But we're going this way." And she headed in the opposite direction. Our new path had us ducking under and sometimes crawling under pipes and projections and squeezing around banks of servers and engines. It took me a moment to figure out what she was doing.

Sandor was leading us around the outer edge of this level, to a point as far away from the airlock as possible, and opposite it. Then she would turn and head across the ship, looking to drive the thing in front of her.

If we didn't come across the septimal with this sweep, she'd back up and push across from another angle. Sooner or later, she'd find it, if the others didn't come across it first.

As it happened, the thing found us.

I heard shouting to our right, echoing off the mounds of metal and the hard floor. The echoes distorted the words, but the voices were high with alarm.

Around the same location I could hear odd scraping noises.

Then a widowmaker bellowed. The bolt shot passed us at an angle that climbed over our heads, but it was a warning.

"It's coming this way," I told Sandor and got my gun ready.

The scraping sounds drew closer. Now I could hear snuffling and low growling, deep in whatever passed for the thing's lungs and belly, a sound that felt like it was travelling through the floor and up through my feet, instead of using soundwaves. No one ever forgot that noise. I'd hoped I'd never hear it again.

Sandor stood feet apart, the gun aimed, the muzzle steady. She was shuddering, her breath shallow.

I caught my gun by the strap and threw it over my shoulder. "Up!" I shouted at her. "Climb!"

Sandor didn't need more encouragement. She threaded her arm and shoulder through the strap of her gun and leapt for the massive engine casing next to her. It wasn't meant to be climbed, but she gripped the flange at the top, hung for a second, then kicked and threw herself upward.

I didn't linger to watch any further. I grabbed the bar of the exterior cage around the whatever piece of engine was next to me and climbed. My feet left the ground and I was reaching for the next handhold when the septimal burst out from the crawl space beneath a tank bolted to the floor beside Sandor's engine. It snapped its mas-

21

sive jaws together, snarling, and threw itself at my dangling feet.

I think I must have levitated up to the top of the casing. I don't remember climbing. My heart thundered, muffling my hearing, as I clung to the top on my hands and knees, panting.

The septimal reared back and took another run at the cage. The blunt head carapace slammed into the casing. The stand rocked and the septimal squealed. It sounded pissed.

I gripped tighter.

Sandor stared at the septimal, her eyes huge and glassy. She wasn't moving. Her throat worked.

I only remembered then the rumors I had heard about septimals in their breeding season being pitted against pleasure dome slaves, for the entertainment of the audience.

As the septimal took another run at the cage I was on, making it shudder and rock on its base, I shouted at Sandor. "Shoot it! Captain, your gun! Drive it away from me!"

The septimal was trying to climb the cage. Its jaws opened, the little center eyes focused on me, as it used its powerful legs and tried to grip with the claws. Septimals were too heavy with muscle to climb well, but they *could* jump.

My heart lurched as the thing leapt and reached for the top of the cage and missed by centimeters. "Sandor!" I shouted again. "Move your ass! Do something!"

She shook her head, blinking. Then she sat up and pulled the rifle over her shoulder and took aim.

The septimal was oblivious to what she was doing. It took another run at the cage and leapt, and I reared up, reaching for my gun as it scrabbled at the cage. It didn't have jointed hands, a small point in my favor. Just sharp slashing claws, one per foot. It slid back, unable to get a grip.

22

Sandor lowered the gun, peering at the septimal with an intense, focused expression.

"What are you waiting for?"

She glanced at me. The same heavy frown. "It's after you."

"Clearly!"

"It's wearing a governor! Check behind its head."

My mouth opened. I risked a glance over the side and threw myself back as the septimal jumped again, its claws swishing far too close to me.

"Get it to turn around," I yelled at her over the creature's intense squeals.

She raised the gun and fired a half bolt. It hit the septimal's back ridge. The septimal spun to face the source and I saw that she was right. There was a metal disk attached to the carapace, fine metal hooks radiating out around the edges of the disk, the tips sunk into the carapace.

But it didn't look like any governor I'd ever seen.

I didn't get a longer look at the device, for the septimal returned to its original quest. It took another run at the cage and rammed into it with its head, rocking me sideways. I hung on grimly as it took a second and third tackle.

"It wants you," Sandor shouted. "You can lead it to the airlock!"

"You want me to be *bait*?"

"Run fast," she advised me.

I spluttered at her.

"It just took a half bolt without flinching," she pointed out. "A full bolt isn't going to stop it. Vacuum will. The thing has a two-hour feeding cycle, Lane. As soon as it gets hungry again, it will go after anything with a pulse, not just you."

"You mean it's *not* hungry right now?" I was appalled. How

much more relentless would it be when it was hungry?

"The governor is directing it," Sandor said. "Right now the governor is telling the thing to get you. You can herd it right into the airlock."

I hated that she was right. "You'll let me get *out* of the airlock before you blow it, right?" I slung the widowmaker over my shoulder then gripped the edge of the cage as the septimal took another bulldozer run at the side of it. There were dents in the heavy-duty piping shielding the delicate machinery inside the cage. "This thing won't let me set foot on the floor. It'll take my leg off at the knee first."

Sandor raised the gun again. "I'll drive it away from the cage, as far as I can with concentrated fire. Then you run."

"Wait, wait!" I held up my hand as she prepared to fire.

She lowered the gun again. "What?"

"Where is the airlock from here?"

She rolled her eyes and pointed. "You can see the hold doors over the top of everything," she added.

I peered. I could see what appeared to be a wall a long way from here—at least it looked like a long way to me right then. The wall was dark, but a lighter patch gleamed in the middle section. The doors, I presumed, and the hold lights beyond. The lights were brighter there because no cargo blocked it, anymore.

"Okay, go!" I shouted at her, gripping the edge of the battered cage I perched upon, ready to throw myself to the floor and run.

Sandor got to her feet, braced herself and brought the gun up to her shoulder. She began firing, aiming the barrage of shots carefully. They herded the septimal backward, a step at a time, while it snarled and raged, until it was forced back behind the housing next to her tank and out of my sight.

"Go now," she muttered, raining fire down upon the thing, pinning it there.

I leapt from the cage, dropped to my feet, and sprinted as fast as I could while twisting and turning around the structures in my way. I would have made better time with a clear path, but so would the septimal.

"Lane, watch out!" Sandor shouted behind me.

The thing had bolted after me.

I kept running, my heart trying to break out of my chest and sweat building under my arms and at my temples. I could hear the thud of its heavy claws behind me, now, which induced me to an even greater speed.

Just ahead, in the gaps between the structures, I glimpsed white light. Cargo hold three.

I burst into the cavernous empty space, my lungs burning, my legs pumping. I could feel the thing right behind me and didn't dare look back.

Sandor had warned the crew. They had the airlock inner door open and Harel stood well to one side.

"Into the lock!" he shouted at me. "Through to the other side. We'll shut the inner doors!"

I kept pounding across the scratched metal floor, heading for the translucent steel room in the far corner. I could see the door with the big wheel standing open. The outer doors were shut tight, or we'd all be breathing vacuum right now.

I could hear the septimal thudding behind me, far too close on my heels for comfort. The stink of it, the basso rumble coming from its guts generated old memories, things I'd thought — hoped — I had forgotten. Severed bodies with faces I'd known. Chewed upon entrails and the stink of human death. It gave me the impetuous I needed to throw myself forward in a last ditch burst of speed.

I shot through the inner door of the airlock and bounced off the cold metal outer door. I used the impetus to push myself at the *other* inner door, this one serving another hold—number two or number four, I presumed. I hit the inner door for that hold as the septimal scrabbled to get its six legs through the human-sized other door. It put the things claws far too close to my heels than I liked.

The door I leaned against opened sluggishly. I slid through and pulled my feet out from between the waving door and the door-frame, snatching them back toward me as the septimal grabbed for them. One claw sliced through the toe of my boot—*silvery pain!*— then I slammed my boots against the door itself, and pushed it closed.

I slithered across the floor and put all my weight and energy into holding the door closed with my feet as the septimal rammed itself against it.

"Lock it!" I screamed at anyone who might be listening. "Shut the damned door! Now!"

The septimal cannoned into the translucent carbon steel once more and this time, starred the material. Cracks ran out to the edges of the door.

"Now!" I shouted hard enough to make my eyes ache.

The door hissed and thudded. The inner wheel turned, as the septimal took another run at it. I could hear it screaming in protest at being denied its target.

Then the outer door clunked and slid aside.

Explosive evacuation—just in case the thing *could* breath vacuum, it would be better to expel it far beyond reach of the ship. Those claws could probably rip through fuselage, too.

I got to my feet, breathing hard. Blood oozed from the sliced open toe of my boot. I stood at the cracked door and watched.

The thing held on even with gale-force winds plucking at it. It slid toward the door, scrabbling with its claws, and hooked the front pair around each side of the doorframe. It heaved with powerful muscles, pulling itself back inside. I could hear it screaming, now, for the explosive roar of the wind dropped as the air left the lock.

From outside the ship, a bolt of bright green/white light took the thing in the thorax.

Rail gun fire.

It jerked. The claws relaxed. It floated away from the ship.

I watched it drift, the legs moving weakly. Then the rail gun opened fire once more and the thing exploded into bits of dark carapace and globs of matter.

I leaned my head against the door and shuddered.

*

"GOVERNORS ARE SHORT RANGE," SANDOR said as she paced the length of the infirmary and back. That was about six of her long steps. "Someone was controlling it. Directing it."

"Someone on the ship?" I asked, remembering the way she had been careful about who might overhear her talking to me. Then I hissed and jerked my foot away from Jones' non-tender touch.

"Just have to seal the wound, and we're done," Jones said cheerfully.

Harel tapped and stepped into the cramped room. "Captain…" He rubbed the back of his neck.

"Let me guess," Sandor said. "The slaver has picked up speed."

I met her gaze.

Harel dropped his hand. "Yeah…how did you know?" He shook his head. "This joker is *not* giving up."

"Clear the room," Sandor said. "I want a word with Lane."

Harel glanced at me. Then he shrugged and backed out. Jones looked like she wanted to protest. Sandor just looked at her. She dropped the sealer and left.

The door shut.

Sandor turned to me. "It's not a slaver."

I nodded.

"You knew?"

"The septimal, the governor...there's other stuff that adds up to it not being a slaver on your ass."

"Whoever they are, they want you bad enough to put on a very expensive operation," Sandor said. "Now the septimal has failed them, they're moving in."

I sighed.

"Who *are* they?" she demanded.

"I'm sorry to say it might be a number of people," I admitted. "You're not the only one in the fringes who thinks I need to be dealt with." I paused. "You can halt and hand me over, then you're free and clear, Captain."

"That's not the way I see it," she replied, her tone cool. "Whoever it is, they want you enough to take down a whole ship while they do it. *My* ship. My passengers."

"What makes you say that?"

She pointed at the wall. Beyond the wall, the ship on their trackers was edging closer. "Whoever it is, they didn't know you'd find a way down to the engine level. They had to presume you were in the passenger sections, two levels up. That thing would have chewed through my crew and then all the passengers, looking for you. From where I stand, this joker owes me."

I picked up the sealer. I'd had practice using one, unfortunately.

So I applied it, closing up the long slash on the top of my foot. "Still easier to hand me over," I said mildly. "Come back at him with all you've got later, when you don't have a ship full of passengers binding your hands. He…she…they're probably counting on you doing just that."

"That's not the way this is going to play out, Lane," she ground out.

I glanced at her curiously. "Oh?"

She nodded infinitesimally. "You're going to have to trust me for the next bit."

*

THE *JAN MAYEN ISLAND* DRIFTED TO a halt and hung, to all appearances lifeless. The passengers were locked in their staterooms. The crew were ordered to theirs, too.

Tipped furniture, shredded cushions, a massive dent in the side of the printer bank made the Courtyard look like a battle ground.

Unfortunately, there was plenty of loose blood to spray around the Courtyard, to add to the effect of a disabled and hurting ship.

The enemy ship came closer and grappled the exterior. We heard the scrape and crunch echoing through the *Jan Mayen.* Sandor winced.

Then a peculiar sucking sound I'd heard only once before. "Vacuum sealed grommet bridge," I murmured.

"They just happened to have one aboard, of course," Sandor said dryly, hefting her widowmaker into a better hold.

"This was always going to be the end play," I told her. "Whoever they are, they want my bones to crow over."

Sandor gave me a peculiar look. "What *did* you do to piss them off so much?"

"When I know who it is, I'll tell you." I straightened up from the wall. I held no guns. "Time to do my bit." I could hear the soft thud of boots on the long central passage, coming this way.

I moved out into the center of the Courtyard, stepping over the artistically splattered blood, and took up my position. It was the longest thirty seconds of my life, standing there waiting for the enemy to show his face.

When he did, I think I sucked all the oxygen in the room down into my lungs with one astonished inhalation. A weak chin, watery blue eyes, a strong overbite. The impression of timidity was offset by the hint of madness in his eyes and his utter ruthlessness, which didn't show except when one brushed up against his ways.

I'd had the misfortune of bumping into him more than once. "Cezário Kozel," I said, as he moved into the center of the Courtyard. He didn't step over the blood. Neither did his men, as they ranged around him…and me.

"Ptolemy Jovan Lane," he intoned. "I didn't expect you to outlast the septimal. I'm kinda pleased you did, though." He glanced at my blood-smeared boot. "Not completely intact, but still able to understand what happens next." He cocked the widowmaker in his hands.

"How many times have I killed you so far, Kozel?"

"Three times too many," Kozel replied. His face tightened. "Do you have any idea how *expensive* rebuilds are these days? Out here in the fringes?"

"Rebuilds are restarts. You shouldn't have remembered a damn thing." But somehow he had, and kept turning up like a bad penny. "Is that why you came after me? You learned I was on the *Jan Mayen Island* and couldn't resist taking another poke at me?"

Kozel laughed. It was not an amused sound. "You don't get it, do you?" he said, when he had himself under control once more. "This wasn't just *chance*, Lane. I've got no patience left for lucky breaks to come my way. This was *planned*, down to the last detail."

I held myself still. If he was as pissed at me as I thought, he wouldn't be able to help himself. He'd spill all the gory details to make me feel as bad and helpless as possible.

"Twenty-three years I've been planning this," Kozel said. "Twenty-three fucking years, you sat in that domed city of yours where I couldn't get at you. But I got you now, don't I?"

"Do you?" I asked with a cold tone.

He waved the widowmaker in my direction but didn't quite aim. Not yet — he wanted to enjoy himself, first. "The only reason you'd move out of that city would be something bad. Something real bad…like an old friend dying. Proper dying, gone forever, no chance of rebuilds."

Horror touched me. "The accident that killed Pasco…that was *your* doing?"

Kozel looked pleased. "*Now* he gets it. Brilliant, huh? Pasco was a spineless freak, anyway. I was glad to deal him the permanent good-bye, 'specially as I knew you'd hot-foot it to Godehaden to split his stuff."

I swallowed. "Which I did," I said softly. "A hundred and seventy-three years of stuff," I added bitterly.

"Ah, it's just stuff," Kozel said dismissively. "But it got you out here, didn't it?" He grinned. "And now —" He bought the widowmaker around in a giant, dramatic swing toward my face, and that was his mistake.

The low energy bolt took him out right between the eyes. I saw it pass over my shoulder from the corner of my eye.

A second bolt, from a different angle, seared through Kozel's hand, destroying the fingers, so the widowmaker clattered to the floor and splashed more blood around.

A third bolt, from the same angle as the first, took Kozel over the heart—what he had for a heart, at least. It spread green light out over his chest, neutralizing the bioelectricity in his body and dropping him to the floor.

"Fourth time's a charm," I told his body, fervently wishing it were so.

Sandor stepped out from her cover, the widowmaker in her hands looking natural and deadly. So did the rest of the officers of her ship, all of them holding two-handers and looking less than happy.

"I suggest you put your guns down and return to your ship and get it the fuck off my hull," Sandor said. "You have sixty seconds, then I will order my crew to open fire upon the intruders in my ship."

They ran. What else could they do? Sandor wasn't playing by their rules.

*

WHEN I SAW WHERE THEY were putting Kozel's body, I caught Sandor's arm. "The nuclear furnace? You could take him back to a parts shop. Claim salvage revenue."

Sandor looked at my hand. I removed it.

"I heard him as well as you, Lane. He keeps coming back at you. Time to end it. I can do that, as Captain. He boarded my ship by force. That gives me leeway. So shut up and watch. I want you to see this."

I watched the crew tilt the hover bed so Kozel's remains slid into the receiving chamber. The shield doors slid down and across and thudded shut. They hissed as they sealed.

Then the exterior indicators switched from green to red, to show the inner chamber door was open. What was in the chamber would last about thirty seconds before it was reduced to atoms.

That was it. Undramatic. Almost silent. But still, my gut clenched, and my heart rate shot up. I looked at Sandor. "Why? You didn't have to."

"I owe you, Lane."

"Not how I see it, from where I'm standing."

"You tried to help, before you knew this was all about you. When you thought it was slavers."

"Ah. I had my reasons for that," I told her.

She glanced around the tiny refuse bay. There wasn't anyone to hear her this time, either. The crew had thrown out the garbage and gone about their business. "The cargo of yours that got tossed. It was your friend's things. The one Kozel killed to make you leave Georgina's Town."

I sighed. "One eighteenth of all he owned," I said heavily.

"One eighteenth? He had a lot of good friends, then," she said.

"He did. He will be missed by more than just me."

She nodded. "That's why I owe you. You tried to help, despite me ejecting your friend's last possessions." She hesitated. "I was wrong about you, Lane. You're a nice man."

"Do me a favor? Don't tell anyone else that," I said gravely. "I have a reputation to keep up—makes my work easier."

"I can see that," she said gravely.

We were silence for a moment, both of us with heavy thoughts.

"How did Kozel remember you, Lane?" Sandor said. "He shouldn't be able to do that. None of us get to remember."

"That's a mystery for another time," I said heavily. I stirred. "I do have one last thing of Pasco's in my personal baggage. A bottle of scotch. Have a drink with me, Captain?"

"Actual scotch? From Scotland?"

"The real thing," I assured her.

"Then yeah, I'll have that drink with you."

We turned and headed for the upper decks.

"You should apply for residency again, Captain," I told her. "That is, if you want to."

"Live in Georgina's Town?" she clarified. "Where weapons are banned, where people smile at each other? Where I can sleep at night without a gun under my pillow? Who wouldn't want that?"

"Then apply again. This time, I'll sponsor you." I cocked at brow at her. "I don't get to decide who gets in, but I have some influence."

"I bet you do." She was smiling, though. It made her cheekbones stand out. "Okay, why?" she demanded.

I stopped in the middle of the passage. This time it was my turn to glance around. Then I opened my shirt and showed her the radiating scar over my heart, with the white disk in the middle.

Stranded

Benjamin Cooper

I didn't know Benjamin Cooper when we first started this process. His story, "Stranded", reminded me of Starship Troopers when I first read it. His characters aren't killing bugs, but the relentless pursuit by overwhelming numbers of enemies with the soldiers just trying to survive long enough to get rescued fell right in line with it. When I offered him one of the spots in the anthology, I was thrilled that he accepted.

If you enjoy "Stranded", you can find out more about Benjamin's work at **https://www.mindofbenjamincooper.com/.**

Enjoy "Stranded". — MP

The transport exploded in midair, bursting apart in a fantastic display of smoke, flames, and twisted metal. The chatter and clanging of equipment being unloaded abruptly ceased.

I blinked at the destruction high above me, the faded pastel sky of planetoid ZD-314 providing a grim backdrop. As if this was merely a minor setback, I spit out my gum and stared intently at the men. The entire company of Interplanetary Marines were captivated, as if watching a fireworks display. A muddled silence added to the uneasiness. We were stranded on an uncharted planet teeming with native inhabitants who were projected to be extremely aggressive.

No reinforcements would be coming. The chances of a transport explosion were astronomically small, an improbable scenario I had failed to consider. The reason, either mechanical or human error, did not matter. Explore Inc., the company that had won the bid for the mission, would never allocate precious fuel stores to deploy the only other transport on the *Pinta*, our base ship, for a rescue. This much had been made clear during the mission briefing. We were doomed, and only the captain, engineer, and I were aware of the dire situation.

The *Pinta* operated under strict governmental guidelines in conjunction with Explore Inc. The company was under enormous pressure to discover more valuable Ultanium for the exponentially expanding human race. Fuel prices were so high, in fact, riots were beginning to break out worldwide. The civilized world was engulfed in an economic collapse of epic proportions. Fuel was scarce and Marines were expendable. Per Explore Inc. policy, planetary system exploration *always* took precedence.

The transport had unloaded the Marines and had been headed back into orbit until the completion of the mission. The takeoff had appeared normal, the high-pitched buzzing of its magnetically powered auxiliary system humming, until disaster struck.

My spectro-goggles lit up with warnings. "Take cover, if practical," the computerized female voice beckoned in my ear, a bit too casually. "Significant falling debris! Impact eminent!"

Jagged pieces of wreckage, some in flames, rained down from the sky. A bolt bounced harmlessly off my camouflaged helmet. When the bombardment was over, I arose from my crouched position with a lofty sigh. My screen flickered. "Hell," I muttered as I slapped the power supply on the back of my helmet, which seemed to help.

"Goggles up!" The red-tinted goggles retracted into my helmet. The wails of the wounded made me queasy. The company had its first casualties of the tour. Hell, some privates had never even fired a round in a combat operation before.

Suddenly, I became aware of the oppressive humidity. The moisture clung to my face like a wet blanket, and the sweltering breeze felt as if I had opened a hot oven. I wiped my eyes with my gloves, smearing dirt on my face. I glanced up to the bleak gray sky to regain some sense of composure. The planet's four grayish moons were staggered on the horizon. There was no time take in the stunning scene. Mustering my courage, I turned to my men.

"Hell," I mumbled, wincing as I surveyed the wreckage.

Several jagged sheets of metal that had made up the hull of the transport had cut through a squad of men like butter. The captain was decapitated, his body a bloody mess. I had been unceremoniously promoted, being next in the chain of command. Another, his leg mangled at the knee, was howling in pain. The insignia on his sleeve identified him as the engineer. Others had been hit by shrapnel. The gruesome carnage was unnerving, but I did my best to maintain composure.

"Medic, stop that engineer's bleeding, now!" I proceeded to relay a barrage of terse orders. Many were in a state of shock. The more battle-hardy veterans sprang into action, aiding their fellow Marines. I tugged at my utility belt, drumming my canteen.

Don't think, act, my instincts cried out.

"We still have a job to do soldiers!" I droned dutifully to no one in particular. "Our families back home are depending on us! Let's hustle!" Best to keep everyone busy until I could formulate a plan; the less the grunts knew the better.

"Secure this landing area! Squad A-1, get this gear out of here!" I barked. "And take this damn rifle off of me!"

"Yes, sir!" A-1 squad leader, nicknamed Sauce, hollered. I momentarily struggled to unsling my weapon before handing it over.

"Goggles down!" My spectro-goggles snapped down over my eyes instantly with a mechanical whir. My vision was suddenly inundated with superimposed data. I cleared my screen, leaving only the map and the order relay scrolling text. "A-3, deploy surveillance drones! The natives will be on top of us soon, especially after all the commotion from this crash!"

"On it, sir!" the A-3 squad leader shouted in my earpiece.

The briefing had made it clear we could not afford to burn more Ultanium if the situation went awry on planetoid ZD-314. They deemed it more cost efficient to allocate their resources testing other high-profile planets for caches of Ultanium. The cost to pay out soldiers' life insurance policies would be minimal. Unemployment was at an all-time high, and the enrollment waiting lists for the Interplanetary Marines were virtually limitless.

Only I knew there was no rescue imminent, rendering the mission irrelevant, but I could not simply ignore the calamitous situation. Despite my best efforts, we were likely going to perish on this alien world. The *Pinta* would be leaving orbit after the next rotation, headed for another planetary target. Time was of the essence. There were two viable choices for our survival: rescue or occupation. Surviving in such a formidable place, one that humanity was not likely to visit again for generations, was a hopeless endeavor. With minimal supplies, our ranks would be ravaged by disease, starvation, and the natives. The question remained: how to convince the *Pinta* to deploy the second transport for our rescue, court-martial be damned.

Men were removing the covers from the turrets and were calibrating the targeting computers. A lizard-like creature with multi-colored fins along its spine and a protruding trunk, skittered in front of me before retreating into the underbrush. Nervously, I adjusted my goggles, again curbing the endless stream of digital relays flashing in my peripheral vision.

Come on, think! Do you want to see your beautiful wife and toddlers again? All they'll know about their father was that he was an I.M. grunt, another casualty of humankind's subjugation of the galaxy.

A Marine apprehensively approached, my screen relay identifying him by his nickname, Munch. "Sir," the private addressed me wearily. "What should I do with the analyzer crates? I'd ask the engineer, but…"

"Cut the sir crap, Munch, we're in a tight spot," I shot back. "Clear out this fluorescent foliage and set it up here." Against protocol, I removed my helmet and scratched my head. If the engineer could be revived long enough to acquire the sample, hit pay dirt, and transmit the data back to the *Pinta*, they'd be forced to send an extraction team in order to preserve the physical sample, as required by Explore Inc. policy.

"Need to see the engineer," I mumbled.

"Engineer Scope is critically injured and currently on sick roll," the computer informed me. Urgently, I rushed to his side. The company medic was attending to him, tightening his tourniquet. I noticed the gauze on his leg and sides had already soaked through with blood. His face was pale, eyes oscillating wildly.

"He coherent, doc?" I asked as Scope's eyes rolled up. I kneeled and leaned in towards his pasty, blood spattered face, with an empathetic smile.

"Stay with me, solider!" I urged. "You can save the whole lot of us! I just need you to fire up that analyzer there," I said, motioning to the massive drill-like mechanism Private Munch was unloading. "It's our only shot at a rescue. If the sample is positive, protocol will force them to acquire it." The doc's eye's widened, realizing their survival hinged on the engineer, the only one qualified to run the analyzer.

"I need the code sequence," Scope said weakly, lips quivering. "New safety protocol from the company."

"What?" I snarled. "I wasn't notified! Who the hell has the code?"

"Get the code," Scope managed to articulate before convulsing into a seizure.

"Hell," I despaired, rubbing my chin in thought. "Explore and their damned red tape!" The odds were becoming insurmountable. Smelling salts failed to rouse him. The medic suggested injecting a shot of adrenaline to jolt him into temporary consciousness. I had to find the Marine with the code before the shot was administered to maximize Scope's time.

Once ordering the medic to secrecy, I paced nervously. Strange cackling sounds emanated from the jungle nearby, over the trilling of insects and bird-like creatures. Some unseen menace was stirring up a ruckus out there. The relentless heat was sapping my energy. My skin felt as if it was crawling, itching under my auto-camouflage armor. The all too familiar feeling of claustrophobia I had developed from deep space travel began creeping in. My clothes felt constricting, and the dense jungle felt as if it was closing in on me. Sweat dripped from my nose as I gasped for air so humid it seemed there was no oxygen in it.

In actuality, there was no constraint, only vastness. ZD-314 was surrounded by several systems of gaseous planets and swaths of empty space separated it from Earth.

Suddenly, I snapped out of it. "Munch, let me ask you somethin'." He immediately dropped the crate he was carrying, rushed over, and saluted.

"What is it, sir?"

"Have you noticed anything out of the ordinary within the ranks?"

"Nothing comes to mind, sir."

"Think again. No detail is too small. Rumors in the barracks? Or chatter at mess? I know you hear plenty at the table since you're there so much."

"Nothing, besides Sly getting extra ration credits. That's how I scored an extra sundae last night, he owed me from a World Series bet." His voice grew excited at the recollection of dessert; twisted, considering the circumstances.

My brow furrowed as I contemplated my next move. The seemingly insignificant lead was all I had to go on. "The enemy will cut our heads off if ya don't help with diggin' those trenches. Re-deploy to the perimeter with Squad B-2, forget the crates."

"Yes, sir!" Munch responded, snapping to attention.

"Where the hell is Sly?" I groaned. My visual readout put the private twenty meters in front of me. I found him assisting in the placement of a fallen tree trunk.

As I approached, a chorus of wild, guttural howls came from the tree line. My stomach dropped. The cries were not human, but from the natives that roamed this untamed world. The briefing had mentioned tribes of nomadic bipeds. My screen lit up with warnings. The drones picked up large swaths of heat signatures gathering near the edge of the jungle. The two automated turrets had just come online and were tracking movement.

"Off-screen!" I snapped. The slew of warnings dissipated, letting me ponder the impossible circumstances. Miraculously, I had to locate the code-master without a company-wide broadcast, since that would be considered treason, per Explore Inc. policy. Then the code would have to be relayed to the engineer, who would have to be resuscitated, all while fending off the enemy. In addition, the sample had to be positive, transmitted to the *Pinta*, and then we still had to hold out for rescue.

"Aww hell," I muttered, defeated. "Company order: All non-essential personnel secure the defensive perimeter! Let's show'em what we're made of, Marines!" I ordered enthusiastically, my voice growing hoarse. With an emphatic wave, I beckoned the men around me to follow as I hustled to the barricade of fallen trees where squad B-3 was feverishly digging in.

"Private Sly!" One of the men stopped working and tossed his spade to the side.

"I was waiting to be relieved. Much obliged!" the slender private responded with a slight Martian accent. I expected him to stiffen at the sight of my stripes, but instead he simply shrugged.

"My bad, boss. What do you need?" Sly asked, rolling his s's as many Martian colonists did, with an attitude far too cavalier for addressing a sergeant.

"If we weren't waist deep in a shit storm right now, I'd reprimand you!" I yelled. Sly maintained his indifference. "But I have bigger problems than your pompous attitude. You've been making extra credits on the side. Talk."

"Talk about what? The weather? Well, we all know it's hot. And don't get me started on these uniforms…"

"Comedian, huh?"

"Yes, sir! Part-time! Imitations are my specialty."

"And let me guess, your set tonight will include an imitation of me." The rest of the squad slowed their work, doing a poor job at pretending not to eavesdrop. "Marine twenty-two, goggles up!" I commanded. Sly's goggles suddenly retracted, much to his surprise.

"Look at me, you cocky worm. I'm not here to reprimand you or weed out contraband," I said, leaning in close, locking eyes with him. Finally, his nonchalant demeanor wavered. I delivered a deep, lasting stare. "Explore is gonna leave us on this pitiful planet to rot if you don't tell me what I need to know."

He pondered this momentarily. "Think I want to spend all year in the brig? I won't ignore a direct order."

"Out with it, soldier," I urged. Instantly, both our spectro-goggles snapped over our eyes, my screen flashing red in an array of alerts. "Perimeter breached, Turret One and Two activated!"

The turrets, perched atop their four meter tripods, began firing at the intrusive hostiles. Instinctively, I dove for cover, pulling a shell-shocked Sly with me.

The blood-curdling cries of the natives echoed over the steady thumping of the automatic, motion-activated turrets, which were shredding the surrounding foliage into salad. Still, the shouts grew louder.

"Let's pour it into 'em boys!" I beckoned before unsheathing my side arm and rising from behind the barricade, all the while cursing my decision to forgo my rifle.

"Push 'em back!" I urged as I blindly emptied multiple rounds into the fray.

The cries of the enemy waned and the staccato of gunfire gradually tapered off, small silos of smoke swirled from the turrets. I did my best to listen over my heavy panting. Hesitantly, I peeked over the rudimentary barricade. Where had they gone? Were they all dead? My spectro-goggles scanned for targets. The seemingly unnatural purple leaves of the shrubbery continued to sway from the onslaught of firepower.

Approximately thirty meters out, a beast emerged from the underbrush. The creature was just over a meter tall with a cat-like face, sleek black fur, gangly arms, and covered only with what appeared to be several strips of leather wrapped around its torso. It spat out some horrid, guttural sounds that were more like monkey shrieks as it shook its jagged spear in my general direction. In a rage, the beast charged. With a mechanical whir, the turrets cut it down mid-stride.

"Hold your fire!" I beckoned. The squad was visibly shaken, except for Sly, his zeal more prominent than ever as he gestured obscenely towards the jungle while unleashing a torrent of profanities. "Hold your position. Another attack is eminent."

"These overgrown stuffed animals don't stand a chance," Sly said evenly.

"Still need that name," I huffed, wiping my brow. The heat was stifling, the humidity suffocating.

"It's Cricket. Satisfied? The weasel wanted protection from the goon squad."

"What the hell kind of nickname is that?" I scoffed. "Is there anyone around here who doesn't have some ridiculous nickname?"

"Well, there's Joe," Sly retorted, answering the rhetorical question. "Joe is that mute in squad C. Some call him Mutie. So never mind, I suppose that counts as a nickname."

"Where the hell is Private Cricket?" I snapped impatiently. My spectro-goggles located his beacon on the right flank. "Be vigilant. They'll be regrouping. They break through, we're all dead."

My uniform seemed to grow heavier with every step, punishment for our unwarranted invasion of this virgin world. The humidity was growing thicker, so thick it felt as if I could almost swim through it. How I longed to be back home in my air-conditioned holo-room! If I ever got back to Earth, I promised myself I'd settle down for good, become a family man once again. No more drinking and gambling. I'd go back to school, perhaps become a programmer.

My goggles locked onto Private Cricket squatting behind a berm of debris. His eyes grew wide as I barreled down on him. I actually saw his lips quiver. His squad spotted me storming in and made way. With both hands, I grabbed him by the vest, yanking him upwards. "Are you the code-master? Where'd you get the credits? If you don't tell me, I'm won't have to court-marital you or let the goon squad institute peer justice, cause we'll all be dead!" My patience had worn thin.

"I needed protection, sir!" an alarmed Cricket pleaded. "They were waking me up at night, drilling me, ridiculing me, urinating in my canteen!" The fresh-faced private from the moon colony sounded absolutely petrified.

"Well, I'm going to piss in your mouth if you don't talk!"

"It was Penny! He gave me a loan for a service rendered. Please, don't reprimand me!" I realized I was literally holding him off the ground, his feet dangling like limp noodles.

"I didn't know it'd be like this!" he whined. "I thought I was being patriotic by signing up! I just wanted to make the galaxy safe for future generations," he explained, sobbing softly.

"Here they come again, boys!" someone hollered.

I released Cricket and he fell to the ground, fumbling for his weapon. Dark faces emerged from the surrounding flora, the growing mist aiding in their concealment. They had managed to infiltrate the perimeter virtually undetected. The turrets automatically targeted and unleashed their fury.

"Get up there, private!" I urged Cricket as he stumbled, before finally resting his rifle on top of a girthy tree trunk.

A single thunderous, bone-chilling shriek was heard. A symphony of cries returned the call, and then suddenly more of them came forward. The savage horde charged, their stumpy legs chugging like pistons, their rudimentary spears waving above them.

"Fire at will!" I ordered, even though many had already begun to fire into the waves of warriors hell-bent on eliminating us, the intruders. The turrets didn't seem to deter their ranks, and another wave pressed the attack. The bullet count in the upper right corner of my goggles plummeted until my clip was empty. Many fell but still they came. With a grunt of aggravation, I loaded another clip. Scores of spears soared through the air. The squad was forced to take cover. I ducked, several spears flying overhead.

"Bigs is down!" someone hollered. Bigs was sprawled out several meters down the line, a wooden spear protruding from his chest, the projectile having found a soft spot in his flak jacket. He clutched the shaft fruitlessly, grimacing. Moments later his arms went limp and his face went slack.

Putting the lost comrade out of my mind, I returned to my grim duty; firing at anything that moved beyond the barricades. The rate of fire slowed across the lines. Reports of casualties scrolled across my screen.

"Turret Two malfunction!" the computer chirped.

"Display perimeter!" I beckoned. The outline of our positions popped up, the red flashing circle indicating the lame turret. "Company order, hold your lines! Squad D-1, reinforce the west barricade!" I watched the green triangles on my screen redeploy to my satisfaction.

Someone yelled, "Incoming!"

I glanced upwards to witness a cloud of spears raining down. I braced myself against the log wall just before they began sporadically falling, many sticking in the ground like flagpoles.

"They're not going to attack again, are they? They're crazy!" Cricket exclaimed. Military strategy dictated the barrage was meant to soften up our lines for yet another assault. Heavy footfalls confirmed it.

Mustering my courage, I once again forced myself up to a defensive position. The scene was a sight to behold. A sea of them were coming at us, shrieking wildly. They leapt and climbed over the scores of dead.

Why do they hate us? I wondered as I skillfully aimed and squeezed off several rounds, the motion-activated bullets finding their targets with ease. My screen flashed yellow, my sidearm communicating wirelessly with my goggles, indicating I was on my last shot. Carefully, I picked out the closest target, one with unusual leathery garments wrapped around its head. He spotted me, advancing as I took the shot, which grazed his shoulder. The thing barely took notice as he continued his push.

"Hell," I muttered as I dropped behind the safety of the berm to reload.

"These things are relentless!"

"The tests have gotta be done by now! Where's our reinforcements?"

"Yeah, where's our ride?" another frightened Marine questioned hysterically.

"Cut the damn chatter!" I ordered. The creature catapulted over the barricades, practically over my head. He landed with a resounding thud. Frantically, I fumbled with a new clip from my ammo belt. Flashing his jagged teeth, he snarled at me as he stomped his bear-like paws. Thankfully, he was unarmed. He paused, spotting a spear stuck in the ground. Instinctively, I lunged for it, my speed belying my bulky frame. It came at me, claws splayed, jagged incisors flashing. I managed to bring the spear up just in time, and my attacker practically impaled himself. He continued to feebly wave his arms at me as I forced the spear deeper, my back pressed against the barricade for leverage. Finally, his eyes rolled up and he was motionless. It took all my strength to push him to the ground.

What fools to use such primitive weapons against a superior force, I thought as I watched the purplish blood bubbling up from his wound.

The enemy was breaking through. Most were cut down by rifle fire, but others were taking Marines down with what looked like tomahawks. Several tense minutes passed before the attack could be repulsed. Marines continued to fire at the shadows beyond the barricades. The defensive perimeter was restored.

The battle was reminiscent of Old Wild West movies from the cinematic archives I watched as a youth, in which hordes of savage Indians battled a handful of cowboys with rifles. The movies always portrayed the Indians as ruthless killers, though I knew better than to label them as such. Still, the stereotype was imbedded in my mind.

Turret One was registering out of ammo. Panic was beginning to spread through the ranks. Another push by the enemy, and our lines could be overrun for good.

I opened the company-wide communications line, barking orders as I hustled to Private Penny's location, near the center of our fortified position. "If you ever want to get out of here, do your jobs, and trust your training! The *Pinta* will be sending the other transport to extract us shortly!"

By the time I reached Private Penny, I was laboring, gulping the hot air. He was casually leaning against a stack of crates labeled *Terraprobe Analyzation Receptacle*.

"We 'bout ready to go home, drink some cold ones, sir?" Penny asked, barely raising a hand in the poorest excuse for a salute I'd ever seen.

"The damn code!" I wheezed, between breaths.

"So, Cricket blabbed about me doing the squad's taxes and insurance forms? Well, I suppose I could handle yours…for a fee, of course."

"You listen up, cockroach," I fumed. "I know you are the code-master. I don't care what orders you have from Explore. We all die if we don't get that transport down here, and it ain't coming unless we get a positive hit."

"They'll revoke my bonus if I divulge my identity," Penny replied, steadfast.

"You just did, you ignorant slime!"

His expression soured. "But isn't Scope dead?"

"He's hanging on," I assured him as the staccato of gunfire rang out, punctuated with screams of agony.

"I didn't sign up for this!" he lamented throwing his hands up in despair. "Why didn't they send combat droids on this mission?"

"Because you're less expensive," I stated flatly. "Even after all the food, training, and other discretionary costs."

"I know," Penny sulked. "We save Explore an average of nine thousand dollars per soldier. That's what they always said at boot camp."

"But you're not here to die. You're here to provide for your family. Am I right?"

"I'm not a fundamentalist colonizer," he admitted. "My base salary barely covers my parents' living expenses. No one will hire an eighty-year-old anymore. And Social Security doesn't pay out until age ninety."

"Well, if you're counting pennies, count on this: if we don't get off this rock your parents will be out on the street once your life insurance runs dry."

"You won't report me for insubordination if we make it out of here?"

"Is this about nullifying your policy? Just type in the damn code, do I make myself clear, Marine?" I bellowed, grabbing the dejected private by the collar and dragging him to the analyzer. The medic was changing Scope's blood-soaked gauze on the gurney.

"We've only got one shot before this poor bastard keels over. Okay doc, let's do this." The despondent medic pressed one hand on Scope's bare chest, holding the needle in the other. With a grunt, he plunged in the needle with enough force to pierce his breastplate. The gravely injured solider let out a wheezy gasp, and his eyes shot open. He looked around, dazed, eyes bloodshot.

"Listen carefully, Marine. The only chance for us to live through this is for you to run the analysis. Fast!"

"But a full spectrum readout takes hours," Scope stammered.

"We have minutes. You better think of a workaround. Otherwise, we're all cat food for those overgrown felines out there." We propped him on a stool in front of the control panel. Seemingly working from muscle memory, his fingers were a blur on the keyboard and joysticks.

"Input the code," he said weakly, struggling to keep his head up. After Penny had punched in the security clearance, Scope got to work. A few seconds later the funnel-shaped device whirred to life and the motor inside roared.

"Ready to extract a sample," he said, grimacing. The rows of green lights atop the cylindrical metallic hull lit up, and the thing began gyrating like mad, the metal support legs vibrating so intensely I thought they might snap.

"Sample has been acquired! Tricky part is speeding up the analysis. Maybe I can bypass standard protocol and fool the system into thinking the sample is stable enough to test the particles. If it doesn't work, it'll explode, incinerating us instantly." Scope's voice was labored, every movement sending him into the throes of agony. I swallowed hard. I noticed Penny take several steps backwards.

An all too familiar chorus of animalistic shrieks ended the brief tranquility. Gunfire grew increasingly louder. The perimeter had been breached in several spots.

"Should be able to isolate the terrra firma, hopefully with Ultanium particles, containing it in the spectro-analytical casing. Once it runs through the preliminary series of electromagnetic resonating transmissions…"

"You can do it, Scope," I urged in the most encouraging tone I could muster. I realized I was rubbing his shoulder.

A serendipitous confluence of events had led to this moment of finality. Scope cringed, his fingers gliding over the touchscreen as if he were creating an unduplicable work of art. "Almost there! The isotope is just about isolated."

Behind me, Penny shifted nervously. "It makes sense to abandon us, from a scarce resources perspective," Penny jabbered anxiously. "I just thought, we all thought, that morally, the company would never do that."

"Come on, you all know corporations have no remorse, no soul. Profit margins run through their veins," I commented, staring eagerly at the analyzer.

"I can't believe it," Scope muttered as the machine chimed. "I bypassed several necessary protocols. But we got a positive! Impossible!"

"Transmit it to the *Pinta* immediately. Hurry!" Scope's fingers were shaking as he battled to remain conscious. "It's done," he said as the tension in his face faded.

"Damn fine job, Marine!" They helped him back down onto the gurney and he collapsed. The casualty numbers were piling up on my screen until a priority transmission flashed across.

"Acting commander Sergeant Fisher, this is Senator Kang on the *Pinta*."

"You better send that transport down if you want to secure that sample! We're under heavy fire!" A cacophony of explosions and screams echoed from all directions.

"Agreed. First, however, we need to ensure your ranks have not been infiltrated. Do have the security clearance code for the new coercion protocol?"

"Aww hell, you gotta be kidding!"

Dagger

David A. Gray

I also didn't know David A. Gray before putting out the call for submissions for Fight or Flight.

Dagger grabbed my attention right away and I knew within a few paragraphs that I'd be offering him a place in the anthology. He's done some great world building and his writing puts you right in the middle of the action. It's great stuff and I really enjoyed it.

If you enjoy "Dagger", you can find out more about David's work at **https:// davidagray.com/.**

Enjoy "Dagger"! — MP

This is my 100th resurrection, and it hurts. I hear some of the old-timers have passed 10,000. No wonder they all have that look in their eye: if I have to relive my most painful memories 10,000 times I'll be a basket case, too. Not that anyone cares, so long as we can still fight. So here I am in the dark dirt, and my caul is dredging up the most awful things that ever happened to me and replaying them, over and over. Every so often I surface for air, like now, then it's back under again.

"We can fix the body of just about any soldier whose caul gets them back, but the decision to *really* live again, that's down to you," a tek said, back when I believed what people told me. I was sitting by the tank, still wet, watching the tiny silver scales of the caul slide back and forth over my uprated body, out through pores to form a near-impenetrable armor, and back in to glide through my bloodstream, tickling my brain and fixing tiny flaws in my toughened organs. I felt like a god.

"When you die," he'd said casually, "and you WILL die, your caul will help bring you back up here," he rapped my stubbly head gently with a knuckle. "But unless you *want* to come back, I mean *really* want to, then you'll drift off, and all we'll be left with is an incredibly expensive zombie. So, your caul will give you a jump-start by reminding you of the really intense stuff."

A jump-start. No way would he have said those exact words. The caul did that, too, I realized: it dumbed-down things or put them in terms you'd relate to, inside your brain, seamlessly. He likely wasn't even speaking the same language as me. I doubt I was even speaking Spanish any more.

So here I am, in the dark, with the worst memories to endure. Maybe if I concentrate I can make it have a sex memory? Faint hope…

*

"SHIT, SAMMY, YOU'RE NOT SERIOUS, are you? We thought you were just messing with us, girl!"

I'd never seen Jojo look worried before, even that time the militia dragged him out for a beating.

"Course I'm serious, boy, what future do we have here?" I waved a hand to take in the stained concrete shacks, the old men sitting around listlessly. "What's for me? Have a kid at 17?"

Jojo looked down, embarrassed. We'd run the streets since we were old enough to toddle, the closest of friends. But we both saw the way the men looked at me now I was 16. And fighter though he was, Jojo wasn't much bigger now than when he was ten, so he couldn't protect me. Not that I *needed* protection, in the main: I carried a wicked blade made of the new space alloy, that would cut through steel, let alone a dodgy old man with rape in mind. But still … for all the changes, life here was short and ugly.

"I know, Sammy, but this? Leaving Earth forever?"

Behind us, in the glassy cube of the recruiting station, an older man sat, watching us with a mix of welcome and sadness. Must have seen this a hundred times, I thought. Some of us had gone as far as the double-door setup they had: there was some kind of scanner in the frame that made an instant evaluation and told you if you were suitable. If you were over 18, pretty much forget it: teens, we had about a one in ten chance of passing whatever it wanted. And me and Jojo had stood there for a dare the moment we saw it. Whatever it looked for, we had it. But we'd never gone through the second door.

"Leaving *what* exactly forever? They just give us trinkets, toys that they think we're ready for! Meanwhile they come and go up there like gods, leaping from star to star! And they've offered us the chance to do the same! Do you want to be like these old men? Sitting around drugged up until you die?"

Flavio bristled: he was from a good family, and well fed, mostly, starting to run to fat even at 16: "It's getting better, Sammy. Nobody goes hungry any more, and they even can cure cancer, now. Why would you leave? It's only going to get better, right?"

A couple of the other kids muttered agreement, but Jojo didn't.

"I'm going," I said, turning to look Jojo in the eye. "And I want you to come with me."

Jojo finally nodded, and we walked in together. I thought that maybe Lari came, too, but for some reason can't remember. Guess I didn't care that much. The outside doors closed and the inside ones opened, and we stepped through.

This should have been a happy memory, me and my beloved Jojo joining up together. But I'm crying like a baby, even though in the darkness I have no body and no tears.

*

BROILER BUST OUT INTO REAL space ten light-seconds early, its 1,000ft-long metal spine screaming protest and the hull deforming and re-flowing as it went from near-absolute zero to incandescent white. Nobody but a fool came out of the wire early, but we were made fools by desperation. There were ships waiting at the end of the wire. Here, if we survived, was our unguarded prey. So, we hung on in our drop bays and listened to the ship groan and howl. A second later the temporary floor thrummed as colossal energy cells drained in a moment, feeding the maulers. An impact, then another, as something fired back, then our cauls stiffened and oriented us for launch. Behind my eyes, a rotating web of lines and icons and information. All but the vital ones faded to pastels: me, the rest of the 100-strong Dagger team, and our target.

"On my mark," Alpha muttered laconically, "three, two…."

He never got to one, as Broiler opened its irises and launched us at gees that would have reduced any un-modded human to jelly. Our cauls were tight reflective silver, covering us, shimmering with shifting energy fields. Inside my body, I felt its cool presence, reinforcing bones that were already strengthened beyond steel, slithering around organs that did the job of heart and lungs and other, new tasks, and cooling the vast new landscapes in my head. I was a god, flying through space, a millionth of a second away from death. *But what kind of god are you, exactly?* a voice in my head whispered.

A swarm of splinters wove through our open ranks like choreographed lightning, ripping open the flanks of the desperately turning prey. Beams lashed out at us, tiny dark stars bloomed, and I mourned comrades. A beam caressed my caul, sending alerts into the red, then we were out of the firing zone, and the dark side of the ship was rushing at me. A hundred fires blazed inside, tiny red pinpricks on the massive dark flank. I rotated and hit feet first, my caul shaping fields so we punched right through, down into the bowels of the stricken vessel.

*

"YOU KNOW WHAT THE TITHE means?" the kindly recruiting officer asked us. Jojo and me looked at each other, and back to her, and shrugged: "Sure we do."

"I don't think you do," he suggested. "You have both been allowed entry, but few applicants have what it takes to pass the training process. If you step through the door behind me, there is no going back: dead or alive, you will belong to the fleet forever."

We knew some of that from the newsfeeds. We'd been babies when the ships had come, and so for us, they'd always been there. I couldn't imagine what it must have been like to have imagined we were alone in the universe, and then to be discovered, and by other humans at that. Humans who flew in 30-mile-long starships, and who lived forever. Who were engaged in a war that had raged for longer than anyone could remember. And who offered technological wonders in exchange for recruits. There was a lot more they weren't telling us then, and it pollutes every memory I have from these days, like a toxic stain. Guess that's why these memories always come back when I'm dead.

"We're in!" I said with more certainty than I felt. She looked at Jojo, who nodded. Poor Jojo: he followed me from love, I now realize.

"Unfortunately, you are not both in," the recruiter said softly.

"The Tithe limit is reached when we add one of you. The only question is, do you both want to come back in a year? Or will one of you stay behind? This is a tough choice." He looked at me, only me, as he said this.

We looked at each other, Jojo and me, and I felt my heart break. Then we spoke at once, words tumbling over each other.

"We both stay behind," I said.

"I stay behind, Sammy goes," Jojo blurted out.

"I go," I heard myself say.

"Sammy goes," Jojo said, then jumped out of his seat and sprinted back out into the grimy street.

I didn't look back, from fear and shame and self-loathing. And excitement. Of course, the recruiter had been lying: it was all part of the test. Jojo could've come, or maybe could never have come. It was all just to make me into the monster they needed me to be.

The door slid shut, leaving me alone with my tears, in a tiny cubicle. A second passed and, ever the impatient asshole, I demanded: "What gives? When..." then a voice said "Promising. Congratulations. Initial modding will start now." Then the world dissolved in agony, bright searing light that seemed to be scorching every cell in my body. By the time I came to, I was in orbit, trying to stand in a body that looked like me, but didn't feel it.

It turns out there wasn't any basic training the way we'd have known it, no boot camp, nothing so old-fashioned or primitive: it was all about whether or not your mind and body had a chance of handling the changes they would have to undergo. And they'd had tens of thousands of years to perfect that process.

*

I CAME TO REST ON a deck deep inside the ship. I didn't know or care what lighting, atmosphere or radiation levels were like: I could see in every spectrum, breathe, re-breathe and scrub my own air indefinitely, and shrug off any environmental hazard. At the same time, though, I could feel the deck through my feet: it was spongy, and warm.

"Follow the markers," Alpha whispered, and I knew where my comrades were, could see them splitting into groups, could feel their cauls vibrating as they encountered the enemy and shredded them with slivers from their upraised arms. We knew everything and nothing: we were there to get something, but I didn't know what. I ran, jumping debris, kicking through a jammed hatch, sprinting faster than anyone on Earth ever had.

An enemy came out right in front of me, marked not as a visual image but as moving vectors and data. I pointed at it, and a hundred tiny needles launched from my glittering finger and it vanished from my data feed. Whether dead, injured or just too slow to catch me, I didn't know: my caul considered it unimportant and so I no longer saw it.

"We're in," Epsilon shouted, and I knew and saw doors and hatches open throughout the ship, as our clever subversives overwhelmed whatever electronic security the ship had. Thousands of the enemy were vented to space and a score of decks were scrubbed clean of life by overloaded powerplants blowing through their safeties and detonating. I topped 60 miles an hour as I ran, eventually skidding to a deck-ripping halt against a dull bronze door twice as high as I stood.

Three comrades arrived, bright blue markers in my vision, and placed their hands against the door, digging their feet into the deck and pushing. I saw their cauls ramp up power and heat output, and could hear, above human levels, metal screeching.

"On three, Gamma," Alpha7 said from behind me. "We will cover, you go in, fast." That was me, this mission: Gamma.

Again, he only got to two: the door suddenly rotated off and up, soldiers staggering and righting themselves. They lit up with fire as a torrent of beams flooded out. One went down, his caul overloading and dropping him to the deck, unmoving. The other two fell to their bellies and sprayed slivers through the door. My caul nudged me into action, and I sprinted forward into the light. Three streams of tiny super-dense projectiles came from behind me, stopping and restarting to avoid my moving body. If any of these hit, I knew my caul would be taking me back in small parts. Whatever air was in here tore and snapped with the rounds' passage.

The fire from inside stopped and the room filled with organic and artificial shrapnel. I kept on running, my target ahead, marked on my display. I was covered in tiny flecks of something dark and warm and sticky.

*

"DAGGER? IS THAT GOOD?" I asked the psych doc cheekily. She and I had hooked up in one of the rare down times we had from training, something she seemed to be keen not to acknowledge, which made me all the more determined to embarrass her with. The fleet didn't seem to care much about such things, in truth, and soldiers, crew, specialists and teks seemed to be involved in just about every combo and relationship I could put a name to, and some I couldn't.

"If you want to be killed as often as possible, then yes," she said, with a raised eyebrow. "You've been judged to possess just the right mix of impulsiveness and rash stupidity to be in a Dagger unit. Your planet is currently rating highly in Swords... which is handy, because we run out of them fast. Others are Shields, Arrows, Spears, and so on. You're the first Dagger. So, congratulations, of a sort, on impending and frequent death."

This was all new to me, which tended to be the fleet's way: in the six months since joining my expanded brain had been crammed full of combat theory and knowledge of devices that I had never seen before. It wasn't like learning, so much as just suddenly knowing things. And we exercised endlessly, not to make us fit, but to learn how to be coordinated in bodies that were faster, stronger and more efficient. Those changes were sometimes overnight, sometimes gradual, as countless tiny machines roamed around inside us, tweaking and modifying. One morning I rolled off my bunk, slipped, and righted myself with so much force that I slammed my face on the wall, breaking my nose. By the time I stumbled to a doc station five minutes later it had set, and the swelling was gone.

I was about to ask what Daggers actually did, and then realized I knew already, I'd just not had cause to think about it before. Daggers were fitted with the caul, and were present in every close assault. I had memories that were not mine, of glittering-suited figures plunging through the atmosphere of a red planet, soaring through space, hacking at shadowy enemies in the fire-blackened bridge of an unrecognized ship. "Cool," I said, and then accessed the "caul" files. I was sick, right there and then, all over my ex-hookup's feet.

*

THERE WERE A DOZEN ENEMY inside the target room, that I saw only as a cubic space not much bigger than a basketball court. They were marked amber, for not immediately dangerous, and were clustered round the target lozenge, a low hollow-topped container. I got all of this is as information, markers, life signs and possible vectors and outcomes. The caul wasn't into the old-fashioned and limited visual spectrum us newbies were used to. "Too limiting, too rooted in pre-training bias and expectations," a caul expert said once, dismissively.

My instruction was, retrieve the target. I saw 11 of the figures around it marked as red, suddenly, but blocked from my fire options. My squad-mates closed in, arms extruding long molecule-thin swords that sliced and stabbed with a spare efficiency. The last figure was pushed back, but not harmed. The cauls were very definite about that.

My target was small, about a foot and a half long, warm and weighed little. I slung the canister from my back and – cognizant of the "organic. delicate" markers on my vision – scooped it into the container and closed it, hearing the stasis hiss and seal it. Anything inside was safe from all but the most extreme impacts: we used big versions sometimes for tough insertions, though they left you blind and deaf, and were regarded as little more than coffins.

I heard Alpha say to the remaining figure: "Tell them!" and then we were gone again, sprinting for the nearest exit point. I sensed comrades falling back towards us from other decks, saw two icons flare red and die, nodded as I recognized their cauls taking over and carrying their corpses back with us.

I was in a non-exposed position, flanked front, sides and back by my team. Whatever we had, the remaining enemy were in a frenzy to stop us taking it and we hosed down every junction we came to, every hatch, every hole and space, with a sleet of tiny exploding projectiles and ravening particle beams. Still, we lost people, one by one. We turned a corner, fast, and Beta fell through a weakened deck into a searing plasma fire that seemed to reach down through half the ship. I could have gone in after her, into the fire, and my caul wouldn't have stopped me, but it warned that the stasis canister would not survive. So, I kept going, and screamed my hate until I lost my voice. Beta's caul eventually went dead. Permie dead.

A dead end, the blank wall of the hull. Keep moving, the cauls urged, and we ran at it, as Broiler peeled it like an apple. We were out, soaring again, numbering 87, of whom 12 were walking. Ahead, Broiler's black sharp shape, 87 tiny holes opening to accommodate our scattered arrival, and closing behind us.

"Made it with 17 seconds to spare. Well done," Alpha muttered, then our cauls reached out energy fields to fix us in place as Broiler shook and roared.

"We're going back in the way we came out," Epsilon said, dread in his voice. As reckless as coming out the wire early was, going back the same way was worse. "Like standing by the railroad tracks as an express passes. And sticking out both arms and grabbing it," I heard it described. It's like that, but not as pleasant. Broiler's realspace engines kicked us off as fast as she could, then the wire drives came on and we caught hold of that express train just ahead of a storm of missiles from the distant vessels.

*

IT TOOK A YEAR TO be ready for the caul. If the changes had happened all at once I'd not have recognized myself, but when you factor in daily grinding change and mods and training, I could truthfully say I knew every bit of the new me. I didn't look so different: more muscled, way faster in every movement, but I had the same impatient frown on my face. My skin was the same dark brown, I even had the same freckles, that for some reason hadn't faded in the ship's lighting. My hair was short, but I could pretty much will it to fall out or be reabsorbed or grow fast, overnight. And of course, I didn't age any more. Inside, I was not the same, though, and marveled at how weak and fragile baseline unmodded humans were. I was pretty sure I could be run over by a bus and walk away, now. I spent most of my time with the other Daggers, to bond. If that means have sex, then sure, I was bonding lots. We chatted, too, mostly about the here and now: we had no contact with Earth, and little news. "Distractions," the trainers said. But there was an edge to it, sometimes: I'd always been good at spotting when people were hiding something.

"This will hurt," the caul specialist said casually. She then grinned unexpectedly: "But what doesn't, right?"

I just stared. Behind her, a tank full of a dully shifting metal. I knew the caul was 100lbs of the smartest engineering the starfaring branch of humanity had devised: a smart but not sentient metal that "lived" inside you, able to do just about anything you needed it to do. And a great many things you didn't know it needed to do.

"It does NOT control you!" we'd been told early on. There were some really strict old prohibitions about humans being in thrall to anything artificial. Even the ships, that seemed so smart, were not sentient the way we knew it. "At any time, you can tell your caul to turn off, and it will," we were told. "Even if doing so kills you, the caul will obey. Do not forget, ever, that you are in charge."

I knew what I had to do: the caul in the tank was cultured to match me exactly. Cost was never something that came up, but we were very much aware that every caul was a colossal investment in rare materials and technology. The year-long wait was for each one to be grown in the ship's massive fabricators. And for us to prove that we wouldn't fail at this stage.

I put my hand in, and held my breath. It felt like nothing. I started to say that, then it flowed through my pores, saturating every cell in my body. I couldn't even scream.

Much later, I came to, as if from the sweetest sleep in my life. I was aware without knowing how, where all my fellow daggers were. I could feel the colossal training ship around me, sense smaller vessels coming and going. I moved to sit up, cautious. My vision swam with lines, vectors, data, probable and possible courses I might take. I lay back down, reeling, saw that my heart was racing, and with a thought, calmed it. I could sense a shared link with my comrades, feel their confusion, amusement, puzzlement, embarrassment as they accidentally shared innermost thoughts, at least two of whose featured me in very detailed and intimate situations. I pictured myself armored, and the caul flowed out and around me, a dull silver second skin. I could see my naked stomach rising and falling with every breath, but at the same time knew I could take a cannon shell to the gut and not blink.

*

WE WERE OUT OF THE belly of Broiler before we'd even adjusted to real-space again. The ship flooded local defenses with fire, wrecking a score of orbitals, and fired us out like railgun rounds. I was Beta now, the new Gamma having possession of the little stasis container. There were 80 of us, rocketing down through thin cold atmosphere to a city on the edge of big landmass surrounded by indigo ocean. The seven whose deaths were messiest were still being resurrected down in the dirt, but the weeks in the wire had allowed the rest of us to be patched up. There'd been a debriefing, a scathing assessment of all we'd done wrong and the few bits we'd gotten right, and I was bumped up to Beta. We'd plugged into room-sized machines that linked to our cauls and carried out invisible repairs, topped up the exotic metals they were forged from and modified them in ways we'd take for granted.

Now, we were curled behind thick curved two-meter discs whose surface plates moved and shifted as our cauls instructed. Fast as we were, hard spears of dark shielded metal passed through our tight ranks as if we were stationary. Miles below, the first of them were impacting with flashes and expanding shock waves. Amber lines crawled up from the ground to be met with delicate green vectors from Broiler. As they touched, our visors flared with a rainbow of effects. One reached us and Theta screeched briefly then tumbled, burning. If the planet had a name, it was judged unimportant to our needs. Above, Broiler executed a breakneck series of maneuvers and unleashed a non-stop cascade of fire. Her hull shifted and slid around like a fish jumping in sunlight as her smart armor adapted and formatted by the millisecond. I'd have said I knew the attack vessel like the back of my own hand, except that the insides changed at will, too, and whole sections were moved around to suit circumstances. I'd come out of my drop hatch on the outside of the belly, returned to the same spot a few minutes later and then a second after that, stepped out into the heart of the ship's armored bridge, or slid straight into the red-lit medical room to be patched up, or passed on down to the "dirt" for serious regrowth or resurrection. I certainly loved the ship, in a way, and she'd been home to our Dagger unit for a year, alongside a hundred crew and shifting rotations of Sword units. Now, she was a tiny and receding blue dot in my visor. I turned my focus to below, tuning in my dropshield's eyes, too, so I could look down through a mile-deep tangle of beams, missiles and projectiles that were all meant to kill me. I can honestly say I was never more alive.

We didn't contribute to the firestorm: while our cauls could do anything from extrude a blade an atom thick that could have sliced clean through an old-style tank like it was butter, to send an endless stream of smart flechettes through the air, or a near-c pellet that would take down an old-style battleship, right now all we had to do was huddle and fall. Broiler had seeded the atmosphere with hundreds of smart drones whose mission was to destroy anything and everything that opposed us, save for the grand building we were plummeting towards. By the time we were a few hundred feet down, and braking, I could see it was a magnificent coiled structure, shrouded in dust clouds from the rolling waves of devastation around it. There were black smears on high points where defenders had been, and even as I plummeted past a delicate spire three thousand feet high, a squad of enemies boiled out the top and sprayed the air with magenta lines. They were dressed in some kind of battle armor, my caul registered, and I was given a fraction of a second to react. With a thought I sent a dozen fingernail-sized antimatter specks at them in curving, baffling trajectories, then I was past and the caul reported with no fanfare that they were no longer a threat. Then I was crashing through a football-pitch-sized crystalline dome and radiating heat like a meteor as my caul's fields slowed me from many times terminal velocity to land feet-first on stone flagstones. From the readouts, I melted two wide-spread footprints into the polished floor.

*

THE SHIPMOTHER WANDERED ALMOST CASUALLY among us, stopping here and there for a word, a pat on a shoulder, a question, always moving. It was our first time aboard the great ship that had sat above Earth since the day the fleet had appeared. Scores of other, smaller vessels, had come and gone on a near-daily basis but the 30-mile long flagship had been a constant lowering presence. As a mark of respect and honor, was the official line, but no-one from Earthside had ever been on it. Its huge bulk, like a misshapen sledgehammer as much as anything else, offered no clues.

Now, at last, we were graduating and had been ferried over, 3,579 strutting, anxious kids from Earth. We kind of clustered in our designations: Swords, Shields, Spears, Arrows, Helms, and us Daggers. We were the smallest group, just 76 of us. I'd been pumped up with self-importance when I first realized how scarce Daggers were, until a dry weapons tek had observed: "Don't need many of you: a little stupid goes a long way." So, we shuffled our feet and tried to stop our nervous thoughts from broadcasting to the others.

It had been three years since I'd put myself ahead of Jojo, and every new intake I'd gone looking for him, with no success. Probably settled down, got a job and was married, I'd told myself. We'd never been allowed back down. And today we'd be assigned, and most likely depart to god-knew-where: the fleet was still not big on telling us stuff. So here I stood in my caul, that right now was a midnight blue with no decoration. The other designations all had versions of it: the Swords were actually heavier and bulkier than us, with twice as much of the super-dense smart metal swilling around inside them, but were slower and, we all thought, kinda dumb. The ship-based specialists in Shield were stuffed with smart augmentations, so they could calculate colossal energy fields and manipulate them with just a thought.

One moment I was in a huddle with Kat and Raahid, then the next their cauls registered polite "make room" requests and the ShipMother was right in front of me, smiling a little. She was barely taller than me, and looked about 50. The old vets, the mega-death ones, as they joked, they said they were all ancient, but the ShipMother predated even them. Her skin was midnight black, her eyes as gray as her hair.

"Sammy, I hear good things about you. A mind full of questions and anger," she murmured. I said nothing, just stared.

"I cannot tell you everything you want to know, but you are ready for more." She smiled, sadly, and I thought I had noticed a flash of true, unintentionally revealed emotion. I was wrong, again: every single thing the ShipMother did was deliberate.

I was about to say something, anything, but my caul popped up an "updating" dot, and it felt as if someone had opened my head up and hosed information in. I linked with the near-AI mind of the great ship, an incomplete, ruined presence, could see the planet below through its eyes. I'd have fallen to my knees if the caul hadn't stiffened for a moment. As great as the step from plain old human to modded had been, then to melding with my caul, this next one was bigger by far.

I could feel tens, hundreds of thousands of cauls in the ship, sense millions of tiny machine minds all laboring, feel scores of vessels bigger than the largest aircraft carrier bobbing way below, coming and going inside the hull, feel the excitement of new vessels being birthed in colossal chambers. And a dim sense of other fleets, unimaginably distant, other great vessels, comradeship.

Also, pain, awareness that the far side of the vessel, the one always faced away from Earth, had a gouge 20 miles long and over a mile deep. A memory of that wound being afire and alive when the fleet was in the wire, the ship mind howling as enemy devices ravened and burned inside. Bodies, tens of thousands, incinerated where they stood, a war going on inside the ship as Swords and Daggers, every other branch, fought deck to deck. Finally, a victory of sorts, but the heart of the fleet fatally wounded by a weapon tailored for this one task. I could feel a desperate sadness and knew the ship would never, could never, travel the wire to other stars again.

A question formed in my head, wordless: what will it do?

An answer not from my caul, but from the ShipMother, also inside my head: "She will stay and fight when they come."

*

EXACTLY 60 OF US HAD made it, smashing through the ceiling and landing in cascades of shattered crystal. The space was immense: easily a half mile in diameter, and hundreds of feet high. Low wide terraces raised a central platform a good 50 feet above the floor, affording a clear view. A few dozen neutral icons flashed atop it. Surrounding us, an ocean of potential hostiles, numbering exactly 565,519: a prime, my caul noted, a significant number here. None were marked immediate targets. This was, I noted, a WTF moment of some magnitude.

"Alpha?" I sent mentally.

"Steady," I got back, with only a small trace of uncertainty. Then to all of us, a mental image of 50 Daggers forming a perfectly circular perimeter, the remaining nine forming up around Alpha, with Gamma by his side, the stasis canister in both hands. We obeyed instantly, our cauls uniformly taking on a black hue so flat and dense we registered in most spectrums as blank spaces. Our arms were out a little and down, fingers splayed. I could sense thousands of slivers shivering in anticipation in their forearm magazines.

Alpha's voice boomed out in the huge space, amplified by his caul. His message was translated for us: unusual, so I assumed it was of prime importance to our survival.

"You broke your word!"

A speaker atop the dais replied, the translation stuttering with what was registered as fear: "We had no option! They came in force, telling us we would be destroyed if we did not allow them passage! There are ten billion lives in this system alone!"

"You broke your word!" Alpha repeated. "The consequences must be seen by all!" Vectors and instructions flashed up and I jogged toward the dais, trailed by Gamma and three others.

The figures caught sight of the stasis container and one started keening, high and loud: "What is in.... no!"

74

Around the vast room, the crowd surged and parted, arguing, uniting, splitting.

Alpha shouted over the noise: "Let this be a lesson."

We reached the top and raised arms to keep the figures there back: I had no idea what they looked like, but had every one plotted and marked on my combat display. Gamma crouched, opening the stasis pod with a mental command. It hissed and a vast low moan echoed around the chamber as the crowd saw the occupant.

"The heir!", "just an infant!", "you would NOT do such a thing!", and more shock, anger, and disbelief, all flashing round the hall. A figure leaped forward on the dais and I moved like lightning, striking it midway up with a balled fist. It crumpled, unmoving. Not a killing blow, I had been ordered.

Down below, a trio of neutral targets flared red as concealed soldiers ran out of the crowd. One thrust a rod at Alpha and a colossal discharge blew a ten-foot crater where they had all stood.

Updating, you are acting Alpha now, my caul advised. *Advise best lesson and act…*

I looked around, at the tiny target that Gamma had lifted in both hands. Back to the ruins of Alpha.

A blade blossomed in my hand and I struck once.

"Elect a new Superior Teir," I said to the vast crowd. "We will return."

I don't recall too much of the return to Broiler. I remember the vast hall alive with cries of fear and despair, and some of excitement. We blasted up the way we'd come using directed fields, and were grabbed by vastly more powerful fields as Broiler blasted overhead a mile away. I think I'd been sick in my caul, but it was instantly smothered and absorbed.

*

"WELCOME BACK, ALPHA." THE SHIPMOTHER, smiling in her sad, wise way. Her contrived, sad, wise way.

"You will assume command of Dagger in Eviscerator."

"I'm not so sure of the ship name," was all I could manage. "But… thanks."

She actually smiled then, for a moment. "The translation of the name does not do it justice. Did you know all of our ships are named in the Enemy's language, based on their deepest, most instinctive fears?" I did not. After all these years, I was used to having godlike abilities but not being aware of the simplest of facts.

"You have a new mission. You will return the way we came, all those years ago."

"No ship has done so since then, though. Will it not alert the enemy?" I knew, now, what they'd been keeping from Earth all this time: that the fleet's desperate flight was traceable, with time, and that the Enemy never gave up. Earth herself was now ringed with orbital fortresses, glittering new moonlets with terrifying weapons. "It could be in a year, it could be in a hundred years," was what Earth had eventually been told.

It was close to 50 years since I joined up, and the planet was enjoying a golden age. Glittering towers scraped the edge of the atmosphere, lifespans were trebled, disease was a thing of the past, as was war. A doomed golden age.

"They are on their way," she said, simply. "Your task is to delay them."

"But Earth's defenses are incredible now…"

"They are. But…"

But.

*

A SHIP TO SHIP ACTION in the wire is as close to hell as you can get. We'd sensed them headed our way, long before they knew we were there. That was all we had: technical superiority. But we used it well. There were five attack ships in all, and one mission: meet them inside the wire, blow them out of it and make sure their ship cores were removed. That way, there was no trace of them, and with luck one of the trillion other wires would become the focus of the search. With a lot of luck.

The first part, all we Daggers could do was hope to survive as the Eviscerator and fellows detonated dirty novas a light-second ahead of us in the pipe. Nothing could destroy the wire: it wasn't a real thing, so much as a path. But we'd discovered that a really *really* big blast applied correctly, could knock ships out into real-space. Hard. Too hard.

I had been unconscious when fired from my drop bay: that was a bad sign. My display was a mess of signals and blanks and I was tumbling, surrounded by millions of pieces of debris. A target lit up close by: a shattered fragment of a giant battleship. I punched through a dozen shredded decks and then had to use fields to melt my way through a bulkhead of sorts. I found the core, burned the stunned suited engineers guarding it, and physically ripped the plum-sized metal sphere out with my hands. Near-impossible to destroy, these things: the suspicion was, they were left-over tech the Enemy had found and used to conquer the stars. No matter, every capital ship they had was guided by one. We prized them too: we'd muffle them, extract every ounce of information then painstakingly extinguish the shrieking intelligence inside them. Once, we'd built a replica of an Enemy ship, torturing a core into playing along. We'd burned an Enemy home planet with that trick: a trillion gone in a nova.

I searched for Eviscerator, saw her tumbling end over end, lashing at a much bigger Enemy that had her grappled close. I could sense hundreds of Swords and Daggers inside the other ship, eating away at its guts, and went full invisible, powering over with an acceleration no ship could have matched. I found my unit, what was left of it, cutting their way into the enemy's bridge, and joined the slaughter. The enemy shipboard soldiers were big and tough and fast. But we were better. I was hit so hard I flew backwards through a bulkhead but was on my feet, smashed ribs re-knitting, firing a blizzard of smart skelfs overhead. Each one was matched to the enemy DNA and would burrow through their armor, deep into their bones. They were nightmares made flesh. Or rather *we* were.

"Back," I ordered my unit, sensing the Eviscerator breaking free. "Take the core, set charges."

We cut our way back, losing a dozen, five permies. Their crippled cauls set their near-endless power reserves to cascade and overload. As we departed the wreck, a handful of explosions as bright as the sun flared through cracks and rents.

I was almost back inside the Eviscerator when a stray random ship -killing railgun missile fired a full second ago from a capital ship on the far side of the pitched battle caught me square in the back. The chances of that happening were, I was informed as it happened, over one billion to one. "Terminal. Not permie," my caul assured me, then I died.

*

SO, I'M BACK. OR WILL be in a moment. It's always like this: like waking from a bad dream, a few seconds of confusion then BAM, it all comes rushing back. Except this time there's something wrong. I can see where I am, it's a standard post-dirt recovery room, but I feel like shit, and I've got about a hundred amber alerts in my vision. I fire a question mark to my caul, and get a succinct: *Healing 73 per cent complete. Emergency resurrection. Proceed with care, but proceed fast.*

I slide off the bench, feel the cold deck under my feet and instinctively summon my caul. It's not quite right, either.

"Where?" I ask out loud, from force of habit, though I've already reached out mentally to link with the ship. First shock: it's not Eviscerator. Second, no-one answers me: usually there's at least a human tek wandering around answering the dumb post-resurrection questions.

Welcome, Alpha. You are aboard the concealed Retribution-class ship Flayer. Message incoming. Stand by.

A wall in the drab room dissolves, and there's a 'gram of the Ship-Mother. She looks tired.

"Welcome back, Sammy. This is me, but a subroutine: the rest of me is occupied with the battle."

Battle?

"You've been dead six months: one of the worst cases I've ever seen."

I look myself over, inside and out, as she talks. I've never heard of anyone being dead more than three months. Chances are I'm all-new, with my personality loaded in. Ah well. Not that I can tell.

The ShipMother is still talking: "They arrived three months after you died. Not your fault: it had to happen someday. And we've been fighting ever since. You were to be woken when the end was near. Look…"

The view is a tangle of shapes and colors and icons. All bad. Earth is surrounded by a debris belt hundreds of miles deep. Wrecked orbital forts drift alongside twisted colossal enemy battleships that dwarf the flagship. There are too many to count. I can sense of thousands of our autonomous unmanned attack ships, most dead and drifting, some still lurking, stealthed.

The flagship is dying, her front half twisted and radiating heat from a million jagged holes.

"The next and final wave is due to arrive in a moment," the Ship-Mother says. "When that happens, we will do what we need, and you will bear witness and leave to join the rest of the fleet."

"You're not coming?" I ask, but realize I'd known that all along. When a ship dies, its ShipMother dies with it.

"What about Earth? How many people did we get off?"

I see figures roll across my vision. A few tens of thousands of suitable teenagers in stasis, the rest abandoned, unable to survive the wire.

"So, surrender?"

"You should know what will happen if you decide they should…"
If I decide?

She continues: "It's not about territory, it's about us. Humans. Look…"

Images fill my head, things that will rob me of a moment's rest so long as I live. I see a planet taken by the enemy, and the unending horrors. The hate, at what we are and what we've done.

"You were Earth's first Dagger. You have died a hundred times for your species. You know suffering, and you know hard choices. You know how those billions will perish. How those closest to you will die."

And she is gone, as the space around the wire insertion point flashes. Millions of tiny glowing points flee the flagship, detonating among the incoming ships. Beams reach back, tearing mile-long chunks off the ship's bow.

Jojo. Among the billions below, Jojo and the perfect family I have imagined in detail all these years. I can't let that happen to him.

"Shipmother, we need to burn hard to reach a nearby wire point," Flayer advises softly. "I am instructed to tell you there are 300 crust-burners positioned around the globe of your home planet. It will be instantaneous."

I have no choice. I never had a choice. And she knew, all along. She made this happen, to make me what I am. I send a signal to Flayer, and then darken the screens.

I scream hate for the ShipMother, for the enemy and for myself, all alone in the dark. And I know my hate will burn for a million years. As they intended.

Plankholder

A Republic of Aquitaine Navy Yarn

Blaze Ward

I've known Blaze Ward for four or five years, now. Not only is he one of the best writers I know, but he's also one of the best people I know. I'm very grateful that he submitted "Plankholder" for Fight or Flight and I really appreciate his take on the relentless enemy.

His Republic of Aquitaine stories are amazing and I'd recommend reading all of them. He's a very prolific writer. You'll have a lot to choose from if you decide to have a look at the rest of his catalogue. Of the 1.4 million words he wrote last year, I'm very happy that he decided to put some of them into Fight or Flight.

If you enjoy "Plankholder", you can find out more about Blaze's work at **https://www.blazeward.com/.**

Enjoy "Plankholder"! — MP

Date of the Republic March 13, 413 Fleet Maintenance Yard, Bordeen

Jack promised himself that he wouldn't cry.

But like so many other promises he had made to himself over the decades, he figured this one was a lost cause, too. Only one thing had ever held him in place, against all odds and emergencies, and it would be ending soon. Today.

Now.

He would be, too, but today wasn't about him. Today, he would be helping retire the old gray lady after they'd come home from one last mission together.

Jack clutched tight at a mug of watered wine and looked around the reception hall. He'd never done something like this, but then he'd gone to space fifty years ago as part of the very first crew that *RAN CT-9071* had ever had, fresh from the builders. He was a Plankholder of the ship. The was the title for the folks that launched a ship into space for the very first time.

The *Republic of Aquitaine* built sturdy ships, but fifty years was a long time and the powers that be had finally decreed that the cargo tug, Jack's home for his entire career, most of his life, was definitely headed for the wrecker.

"You're doing fine," a voice intruded on Jack's mourning, causing his flinch to nearly spill his wine, which would never do, as he was in his very best uniform.

Tailored, of course, because they never fit. When a man was one hundred and ninety-one centimeters tall, he was supposed to weigh more than eighty-two kilograms, but Jack had been this weight since he was seventeen. Even basic training and technical school hadn't put on more than three kilos, and those had come right back off when he graduated and took his first job as an engineering punk aboard a brand new cargo tug that still smelled like ozone from all the welding and the paint used to make it pretty.

"I don't feel fine," Jack said quietly back, but the woman in front of him when he turned around was Calogera. Master Chief Calogera Vespa. Chief of the Boat of *CT-9071*, at least for a few more hours.

And young enough to be his daughter, in spite of being his boss.

But everyone was too young.

Jack glanced down at his left cuff, on the side holding the wine, and noted four stripes, because Fleet hadn't yet had the ceremony where they awarded him his fifth. Fifty years in service. All of it aboard *CT-9071*. The only times he had left had been half a year of engineering refresher when they put the ship in for a full refurb and update after that damned pirate from *Corynthe* had designed a new fleet for First Centurion Keller and *everyone* had to learn new systems. That and a weekend here or there while the ship was in port or being refueled.

But even then, an engineer like Jack was always needed to help the station crew, since nobody else knew those systems like he did.

"Just keep your mouth shut, your chin up, and your eyes smiling, Senior Chief," Calogera said firmly. "It will be over soon enough."

"Then what, damn it?" he asked, trying to keep from letting his voice rise above a whisper. "What do I do tomorrow?"

She'd been a great boss. Better than a lot of them, and he'd known too many Master Chiefs as Chiefs of the Boat on *CT-9071* over the last fifty years. Jack didn't want to raise his voice, but he couldn't help it.

Hopefully, none of the brass over in the other corners had heard. Or maybe they were just pretending to ignore him.

That would be fine. They'd been ignoring him for a long enough time, just letting him do his job.

"What do you want from tomorrow, Jack?" Calogera asked bluntly, getting right up in his face now.

Or chest, anyway. She was normal sized for a woman, so a head shorter than Jack. Almost outweighed him, but it was all muscle and mean, like any good Master Chief. One of the reasons he'd never applied for a promotion and a new billet. A whole set of headaches he didn't want.

"I don't know," he said, quieter. In his own head, it almost came out as a whimper, but he couldn't help it. "I've been with this boat since the beginning. Hell, I was already serving aboard her when you were born, Master Chief. I don't know anything else."

"Look around you, Jack," she said, turning now and taking his arm. She gestured at the crowd.

The room wasn't packed, but there were maybe a hundred and fifty people in here, all of them dressed in their best uniforms. Command Centurion Sang Kwan, the boss. Command Centurion Nita Jughashvili, the former boss who Kwan had replaced two years ago.

There was even a Fleet Machinist over in the opposite corner, talking with someone that had his back to Jack right now. Once upon a time, they'd been called Fleet Engineering Lords, back before Jessica Keller had totally upended the *RAN* for good in 393. Gods, had it really been twenty years ago?

After that, everyone was a Fleet Centurion instead of a Fleet Lord. Sometime in the last five years, Fleet Engineering Centurion had given way to *Fleet Machinist*. Another mark of the times that were changing.

Jack really didn't want to think about the man over there in the Fleet Machinist uniform. It seemed like only yesterday that a young-punk Centurion named Frode Holt had reported aboard the gray lady to take over as Chief Engineer. And now he was a Fleet Machinist.

"These people are here for you, Jack," Calogera was saying. "For *CT-9071* as she's going to be retired. Normally, they just sail a boat like this to a base, unload all her crew, and shut down the reactors until a breaker tug comes and hauls them off to the yard."

Jack felt tears and blinked really hard to hold them at bay.

"*CT-9071* is getting a send-off worthy of a dreadnaught or a Star Controller, Jack," the Chief said. "That's because of you."

"I know," he whispered. "I'm just feeling my age tonight. We've beat everyone, you know. *Fribourg. Buran. Salonnia.* Hell, even *Corynthe* once Keller took over and started knocking heads together. And in the end its all for nothing."

"Time," Calogera said quietly, finally understanding from the way her face softened now. "The one enemy you cannot defeat."

"The most relentless foe of all," Jack agreed. "Getting old."

She nodded, this middle-aged woman young enough to be his daughter, and put a hand on his arm.

"Just smile for now, Senior Chief," she said. "Tomorrow, you can let it all out. But let the gray lady have her day."

She was gone, even as Jack drew a heavy breath to argue with her. Or hold in the tears. Something. He took a heavy drink of the wine, happy that it had been cut with so much water that it really wasn't much more than grape juice now.

Jack was contemplating going for another mug when a second shadow appeared in front of him. This one was as tall as Jack, which was uncommon in the *Republic of Aquitaine Navy.*

Then Jack did a double-take as he recognized the uniform. Everyone in here was in their best, but only one uniform included a long, black trenchcoat, even indoors.

Jack snapped to and fought not to salute the First Lord of the Aquitaine Fleet.

All the other Fleet Lords and First Fleet Lords were gone, but the politicians had kept their titles. Seven Lords of the Fleet in charge of everything, and this man at the head of the line.

"Relax, Senior Chief," First Lord Whughy said with a helpful smile. "It's not that painful a thing to have to witness, in spite of you never having had to face it. My battlecruiser *Stralsund* had to be rebuilt after *First Ballard* because she'd taken so much damage. They put her back together, but it cut twenty years off her life and one of the first orders I issued as First Lord was to have her retired. Every ship grows too old to maintain."

"First Lord," Jack muttered, uncomfortably.

Too old to maintain described a lot of things on his mind right now. None of them pleasant, or appropriate to bring up with the man who was everybody's boss.

"I've read your file, Senior Chief," the man said, causing Jack's stomach to sink and turn cold. "What kind of name is Volodymyr Palahniuk, anyway?"

"Ukrainian," Jack responded automatically, like he had for fifty-some years. "Just call me Jack."

The First Lord only got the pronunciation close, but Jack had barely said it aloud in a generation.

Easier to just be *Jack* and be done with it.

"Jack."

One hand reached out now, fingers apparently perfectly manicured, as opposed to having grease permanently under his nails and cuticles like Jack did, and tapped a medal that Jack had been ordered to break out of his footlocker for tonight. Otherwise, he'd have left it there like he always did.

"Republic Cross," the First Lord said in an impressed tone. "Tell me about the *Battle of Auspex*, Senior Chief."

Jack wondered how much the man knew. But then, he said he'd read the file. Plus, he was the First Lord, so the man had to be smart. Capable. Tough.

Jack took a breath to calm himself, wondering if he was a show pony right now. The only other enlisted folks in the room tonight were all transferring off *CT-9071*, and that was only a couple dozen people. The other hundred were brass.

"Year of the Republic 371," Jack replied, falling back into himself and his memory.

He'd had to tell the story a lot in the early days, until he stopped wearing the medal unless otherwise ordered. Like tonight. After so long, though, the words were still automatic.

"We were running with a convoy out of *Plinkek*," Jack said. "One revenue cutter as escort for a handful of civilian freighters. *CT-9071* was attached, with a cargo pod in the aft slot and a q-pod under our belly. *Fribourg* had been raiding a lot that year, so everyone was a little tense. They hit us just as we dropped out of jump, clear out at the edge of the gravity well and too far away for the station to engage. They scrambled fighters, but we had to hold off a trio of frigates until help could arrive."

"Q-pod?" the First Lord asked.

As if he didn't know or something. But then, the man had been on cruisers and such his whole career, rather than on the support side of things. At least until much later.

"Looks like a cargo pod from the outside," Jack said. "When trouble arrives, you blow a bunch of fake panels and open missile bays. Tug's got the firepower of an old *Founder-class* Heavy Cruiser when you do that."

"So they came up from behind," First Lord prompted him.

"We were second to last in line," Jack said. "Biggest target, so the raiders came after us first. Probably figured we had more guns than a revenue cutter, too. But they were expecting two cargo pods when they got there."

Jack felt the smile take over his face. First Lord would have been a kid, maybe just in high school on that day, forty-two years ago.

"Command Centurion Castleveddi orders the pod gunners to engage, so they pop everything and hammer the living shit out of the closest bastard," Jack said, forgetting to watch his language around important people as he got caught up.

They didn't give out the Republic Cross for little things.

"She tears him a new arsehole with the first salvo, but then something goes wrong," Jack continued. "Explosion rocks the inside of the q-pod and we think that a missile snuck through. Barn Owl like they used to use in the old days."

"But you had a saboteur," First Lord nodded.

"Yeah, that came out later, when security killed the guy as he was planting his second bomb, but right now all our pod guns have gone silent," Jack nodded. "No answer from the engineering bay when we call. Other teams are launching from two missile tubes as fast as they can cycle, but that's just enough to entertain a *Fribourg* frigate in those days. Same with the four Type-3 beams *9071* has. Tickle him when he gets too close, but not enough to stop if they want to hose us down with primaries."

Jack fell silent. Felt like he was bragging, until he remembered that the man in front of him had once sailed a *Warrior-class* battlecruiser into the teeth of an Imperial Battleship being flown by the old Red Admiral Wachturm.

And won.

"What did you do, Senior Chief?" First Lord verbally poked Jack now.

Jack felt his stomach flip flop and he was back on the deck of old *9071* again, looking at his Chief and saying the dumbest thing he could think of.

I've got an idea.

"The bomb had taken out the engineering controls on the pod," Jack said. "Same time it killed or disabled everyone above the rank of Landsman. So, I grabbed a bunch of tools and cables and all the marines Castleveddi would let me take to carry shit and we boarded the pod. Didn't know what was going on, and it was one of the women with me who eventually killed the bomber. Right then we needed power or we were all dead meat, and I was crazy enough to try it."

"You manually controlled six generators by yourself with nothing but spanners and hammers, in order to route power back to the gunners," First Lord filled in when Jack fell silent. "While commanding the marines hunting down the enemy agent. While fighting a pitched battle with the two remaining frigates, who had gotten too close when the pod stopped firing, expecting that their infiltrator had been successful and that you would have to surrender or be destroyed."

"Yes, sir," Jack agreed.

He wasn't used to Command officers who understood engineering, but this was First Lord Whughy, the man who had invented the Pulse-Two, as well as the Forward Base Administrator on *Keller's Expedition* into *Buran* space.

Man knew his stuff.

"Your actions saved the ship, the convoy, and caused the surrender of two Fribourg frigates, with the third one managing to limp off and escape, but only after *CT-9071* had mauled the living shit out of it first, Senior Chief," First Lord Whughy said.

Jack nodded to the man.

Jack's jaw dropped when the man stepped back and saluted. Him. The First Lord.

Shit.

Jack fought back the tears again.

Didn't help, talking about old battles. They were old.

He was old.

There was nobody else in this room with four stripes. Even the First Lord had retired and become a civilian in order to be promoted.

What the hell did Jack have left after they sent the only home he'd ever known to the breaker yard?

First Lord seemed to understand. Rather than speak, he stepped back with a warm nod and vanished into the crowd.

Jack said fuck it and went for more wine, wondering if he should tell the grandkids minding the counter not to add any water this time, just so he could be numb by the time the ceremony occurred. He was already going to be crying. Hopefully, they'd let him sit in the corner with his memories.

His ghosts. Every kid that had ever served with him down in the engineering bays, including the ones that never made it home from places like *Auspex.*

Nita Jughashvili was at his elbow as the youngster gave Jack his watered wine.

Retired Command Centurion Jughashvili, the boss before Kwan. Still in her dress blacks though, because this was an official thing and she'd been invited along with every other CC they could reach.

Jack flinched when he considered just how few of his former Command Centurions were still among the living.

That most implacable enemy. The most relentless foe. The one who'd taken them all from him.

Taken everything from him.

"Breathe, Jack," she said simply, taking his elbow and pulling him off to one side. Like him, she had a glass of wine in her off hand.

"Sir?" Jack asked, a little sniffly right now, but there was nothing anybody could do about that.

Old age had come for so many, including the gray lady, and Jack figured he'd be next.

What the hell did an old gearhead like him do once they retired him out of service and put him on a beach somewhere? Not like he had any other hobbies. Power systems and life support had been his entire life, keeping *9071* going long past the point when maybe they should have retired her.

But every year, she'd been on the rolls for another budget cycle, even after all of her sisters had been sold off or broken.

"First Lord wanted me to talk to you, Jack," she said quietly.

Jack went cold all over, like he could already hear her words before they were spoken.

What more do you people want from me? I've already given you everything I have!

But he didn't say that out loud. Nita had been his commanding officer. And one of the best he'd known.

He fought to remain still.

"There's going to be a ceremony," Nita said.

"Know that," Jack snapped, biting off the words. "That's why we're here."

"He wants to do something special, Jack," Nita continued. "He's going to call you to the stage to be part of it, so my job is to remind you not to get drunk until later. And not to be surprised when he does. Can you do that for me?"

Jack nodded. She could still command him. That was part of what made him who he was. Lots of people in here could give him orders, since he was just a Senior Chief in charge of Engineering on a boat no longer going to be part of the Navy when this was all over.

Jack sniffled hard to keep everything inside and nodded. Ground his teeth so she didn't hear them rattle in his skull.

It was Nita. Another one young enough to be his daughter. But there weren't that many people in here who weren't.

He could do that for her.

Still, Jack put away half the glass of watery grape juice in one go.

Anything to calm his stomach and nerves.

None of it meant anything at the end of the day. We all grow up, and then we grow old.

"You'll do fine, Jack," Nita said, but then she left him alone, maybe understanding that he needed some quiet time.

Extroverts didn't become engineers. They went into Command or maybe Security. The crazy ones used to fly snubfighters, when that was still a viable job.

Before that damned pirate had invented a new future. Him and Lady Moirrey.

But it was a better future. Jack had to give them that. Peace and everything. Way less piracy from strange ships flying around hitting convoys these days. More smuggling, but that just meant that CT-9071 was hauling stuff between stations or maybe the occasional diplomatic pod hauling important people to some event in style. It had been fifteen years since the last time they'd strapped on a combat pod, and the only time they'd had an assault pod in the last decade had been to transport a whole cohort of infantry to some special competition on *Ladaux*.

Jack walked deliberately to the far corner of the room now, finding the last seat in the last row, and then moving inward one just so he could claim them both and hopefully nobody would want to bother him. He tried giving off all the negative waves, and most people just sort of nodded at him with a bland smile.

He would not cry. Not now. Not in front of all of these people who had come to say goodbye to the old lady. He would do her justice. Tomorrow, he'd find a quiet place, or lock himself in his room and let it all out.

What the hell do you do with the rest of your life?

Jack didn't know. Hopefully the same gods that had let him build a life on *9071* would show him a sign in the morning.

First Lord was moving up to the stage with Sang Kwan. The crowd started filling all the seats.

Jack didn't—quite—growl at anyone coming close, but it was a near thing. He ended up with four empty seats at the end and nobody in the row directly ahead of him.

That was probably as good as it was going to get.

He took a deep breath and held in the sigh that wanted to come out.

Tomorrow.

You can have me tomorrow, you bastards, but not tonight, damn it.

He ground his teeth together to the point that the top of his head hurt, but he managed to hold it all together as the First Lord stood up there, with Command Centurion Kwan standing beside him.

That most relentless foe had won another battle in the eternal war against entropy.

CT-9071 was going to be retired. Stricken.

Just like Jack was, one of these days.

"My friends, thank you for joining me tonight," First Lord began in a voice used to addressing auditoriums full of folks. Sharp and clear, enunciating everything like a razor blade. "I know you have come for the retirement ceremony, but I have one small thing to take care of first, if you will indulge me."

Jack suppressed a snort. There were no civilians in this room. Just *RAN*, active or retired. First Lord of the Fleet was everybody's boss. He gave the orders that everyone else followed, right up to the point that the Senate decided to get involved personally, but nothing like that had happened since Keller and *The Expedition*.

"Senior Chief Jack Palahniuk, would you join me on the stage, please?" Whughy called out now.

Damned good thing Nita had warned him. Jack set his mug down and rose with as much dignity as these old bones could manage. Sixty-eight wasn't as spry as eighteen, no matter what lies he might have told people along the way.

Adrenaline helped. That surge of raw power in his belly like fear. Like he was back at *Auspex*, screaming invective and profanities at a set of generators, knowing that he was the only thing between death and victory for the convoy and every one of his friends.

He walked with his head up and his shoulders back. He was *RAN*, damn it, and had worn this uniform longer than most of these punks had been alive. Even the punks he liked.

First Lord Arott Whughy could have gone into vids. He had that cleft chin and those perfect cheekbones. Jack was tall and skinny and had a face that didn't make milk curdle, but that was about as far as he was willing to admit.

Still, he stepped up on the opposite side of CC Kwan and came to parade rest.

"No, Jack," First Lord said, stepping back and gesturing Jack to slide over. "You in the middle."

Jack managed to unlock his knees and keep them from knocking as he moved over, finding himself between Kwan and Whughy now.

What the hell were they up to?

Jack came to attention now and found a spot on the wall just below the upper weld to concentrate on. He felt the other two step closer now.

"It's not often this situation presents itself," First Lord was speaking again. "And I had to overrule both Third Lord and Seventh Lord on this one. Not without some grumbling on their part."

Third Lord of the Fleet, Personnel: Seventh Lord, Logistics and Supply. Technically Jack's boss, since the war fleets came under First and Second Lords.

But those titles were all from a previous era, just like Jack. Holdovers who would be renamed, same as now you had Fleet Machinists.

Yesterday.

The audience seemed to be in First Lord's hand, chuckling with a joke Jack didn't get, but he was like that. You had to be a politician to make it that far, in addition to being a pretty famous commander.

"However, I insisted, and the only people technically able to overrule me chose not to," Whughy was saying, leaving Jack utterly perplexed.

But he held his attention like this was an annual inspection of his engineering spaces. Maybe not spotless, but running perfectly, every damned time. He had six Excellence Reports, big letter-*E*s painted on the wall over his head to show for it.

Jack did wonder who might pull rank on First Lord. That would have to be Senators. And important ones, at that.

What the hell was going on?

"And so, my friends, I would like to take this moment to celebrate another important milestone in the *Republic of Aquitaine Navy*," Whughy said, stepping back and to one side, clear out of Jack's peripheral vision. "Command Centurion Kwan, you have the flag."

"I have the flag," Kwan echoed a moment later.

He was now in charge.

"Senior Chief Volodymyr *Jack* Palahniuk, you will present your left arm," Kwan ordered.

Jack did so before his brain caught up with him, holding it out not quite level with the deck, but close.

And not even shaking, which was a less-obvious thing.

Kwan took hold of Jack's wrist and pinned a fifth stripe in place.

Jack finally understood.

Fifty years active-duty service. Most people did six years and left. A few lifers went twenty or maybe thirty.

Jack had been in since Year of the Republic 363.

Fifty years, all of it sailing on *CT-9071*.

"At ease, Senior Chief," Kwan called, and Jack fell into parade rest automatically, still not entirely present.

But he'd promised Nita that he wouldn't cry until tomorrow. While he might fail himself, he wouldn't fail her. She'd believed in him.

The audience applauded. Hoots and cheers erupted in more than one place, but Jack refused to even look at the audience right now. This was not his night.

It belonged to the gray lady.

"First Lord, you have the flag," he heard Kwan say under the noise.

"I have the flag," Whughy replied and stepped forward again to where he was a blur in the corner of Jack's eye.

Hands came up after too long a wait and the folks in the audience finally started acting like officers and crew again, instead of rowdy rugby fans.

"That's why I overruled the others," First Lord said to the room now. Warm, friendly. "Jack's been with us for a very long time, and I wanted to make sure that he knew how much we as a Navy appreciated him. Because tonight is one of those things that the Lords of the Fleet take seriously. Just as we are there to celebrate commissioning ceremonies of new vessels, so it is incumbent on us to be there for decommissionings. To mark the endings."

He stopped there and Jack managed to draw a breath, but he knew that there would be tears running down his face pretty damned quick.

"My friends, tonight we are looking at the Cargo Tug *CT-9071*," First Lord continued, like he couldn't hear Jack sniffling beside him. "Like Jack, she has served with us for fifty years. Jack has the singular honor of being the only plankholder still in the service, as he was first assigned fresh out of engineering school, a clumsy Landsman who quickly impressed everyone with his skill, his acumen, and his willingness to go above and beyond the call of duty."

He stopped talking and Jack glanced that way as the First Lord turned and gestured.

"On his watch, the crew was awarded Excellence six times," the man said. "Jack has four combat badges, plus the Republic Cross and the Order of Merit. These are the marks of the men and women who exemplify the best in all of us."

It was true. Parts of it, anyway. Jack had always done what he thought was the right thing. And he had survived, so they had given him a couple of medals for it. And a fifth stripe.

And tomorrow, it was all going away, when CC Kwan ordered him to shut down the various engines, reactors, and generators, prior to someone dragging the gray lady off to a breaker yard and erasing fifty years of hard work and more lives than Jack wanted to contemplate.

The room went blurry, but he couldn't help it. The tears would no longer be contained, regardless of his opinion on the topic. At least Kwan had the sniffles too from the sound of it. Maybe it was contagious, like all those things they warned you about not doing on port calls in strange places.

That, at least, brought a hint of a smile to Jack's face. For a ghost of an eyeblink.

"And now, my friends, it is time to bring things to an ending." First Lord Whughy turned serious. Stentorian, even, filling the room with his voice. "Command Centurion Kwan, as *CT-9071* is to be retired from active duty, you are relieved."

"I stand relieved," Kwan replied with equal dignity.

Jack heard the man turn and march away, but it was difficult to understand, because the crowd in front of him had suddenly grown restless. Gasps and mutterings. Something was wrong, but Jack had never been here before. Never seen the ceremony to know what had just happened.

Wasn't the Command Centurion *supposed* to turn over command to someone else?

But there was nobody up here except the First Lord.

"Senior Chief Jack Palahniuk, you will step forward and raise your right hand," First Lord ordered.

Jack was on autopilot, so he did.

The crowd got noisier. Rowdier, even, but Jack was a man in an escape pod, completely lost and surrounded by endless nothing.

"By order of the Senate of Aquitaine, on this day signed by Senator Tedrik Kasum, Premier, and Arott Whughy, First Lord of the Fleet, we declare to all that Senior Chief Jack Palahniuk of the planet Royko is hereby promoted to the rank of Master Chief. May he exercise this responsibility with authority, intellect, and care, for he is our representative in all things."

Folks started to cheer, but First Lord actually stomped his foot on the hollow deck of the stage loud enough to cut them off. An awkward silence fell, save for the pounding in Jack's ears as his heart tried to decide if it was going to explode or not.

"Master Chief Palahniuk, it is further ordered that you will brevet to the rank of Command Centurion and take command of the Cargo Transport *9071* for her final voyage."

There were probably more words spoken, but they were lost in the roar in Jack's ears and the cheering coming from the audience. The wild howling and excitement.

First Lord had just put him in charge. Jack was at a loss for words. For even rational thought. And blind from the tears pouring down his face.

A shadow stepped close and spoke with the First Lord's voice.

"You'll do fine, Jack," the man said. "And she deserves no less."

Jack nodded. Maybe. Twitched in a way that could be interpreted that way if you were feeling benevolent.

First Lord yelled until everyone shut up again. That took a little while. Jack concentrated on breathing in the meantime, hoping he wouldn't just fall over dead right now. Tears stained the front of his uniform and refused to stop.

"Finally," Whughy said when the people sat their stupid asses down and shut up again. "I have been instructed by the Fourth Lord of the Fleet that I am *required* to transfer Master Chief Jack to his staff afterwards, where he will begin training the next generation of sailors on what it means to be *Republic of Aquitaine Navy*, until such time as he earns his sixth stripe, and then considers retiring."

Bedlam.

Jack felt the First Lord take his elbow and guide him towards the steps now, walking him carefully down so he didn't trip and break his fool neck.

Nita was there with a hug when the mob engulfed him. Calogera, too. Even CC Kwan got in on the act.

Everyone touched him or patted his back. Something.

It was a death in the family, but they were all celebrating, so Jack supposed he could, too.

That one foe that nobody could beat, but God damn it, he was going to try.

Sixth stripe? Just you watch me.

Ten years to teach these kids the right way? You betcha.

And hopefully his name would live on in the lives he touched, the students he sent out there. If they didn't forget Master Chief Jack, then they wouldn't forget *CT-9071*, either.

The gray lady deserved no less.

.

The Sentry

Clayton Scott

Clayton Scott is one of my favorite writers. I've edited a bunch of his work and I never tire of reading his stuff. "The Sentry" is no exception and I knew, even before I read it, that I'd be offering him a place in Fight or Flight.

"The Sentry" brings to mind The Terminator and the Borg — and perfectly embodies the relentless enemy that I had in mind. As Kyle Reese says, "It can't be bargained with. It can't be reasoned with. It doesn't feel pity, or remorse, or fear! And it absolutely will not stop, ever, until you are dead!"

If you enjoy "The Sentry", you can find out more about Clayton's work at **https://terralost.com/.**

Enjoy "The Sentry"!

Chapter One

C'mon, Lork, were you asleep at the controls or something?" Jed asked, his voice echoing from his head being buried within the open console near the starboard wing of the freighter.

"Asleep at the controls, Jedidiah Kramer? At least the ship is still intact!"

"I thought your evasive maneuvers were better than that!"

"I would not have needed evasive maneuvers if you had provided that Federation Security Officer with the appropriate clearance codes."

"I can't provide what I don't have, Lork," Jed replied, twisting slightly to get a better look, deeper inside the ship. "Man, I think engine two's reserve fuel tank is ruptured. And I'm never going to buff out these scorch marks."

"Perhaps next time you can refrain from directing one of your foul Earthen insults at the man in the ship with the large weapons systems?"

"Foul Earthen insults? I'll have you know that the human body is a beautiful thing and the word I used was just—"

"Hold on!" Lork interjected, his voice tinny over the ship's internal communications array. "I think you will want to return to your seat, Captain."

"I'm not a freaking captain, Lork," Jed replied, prying himself free of the internal systems of the ship. Propping himself up on his knees, he brushed dirt from his jacket sleeves and wiped a shine of grime from his dark flesh using the back of a gloved hand.

"Captain or not, you are the owner of this ship, and I think you're going to want to see this!"

"Give me just a second," Jed said and reached over, grabbing the metallic cover to the opening he'd made in order to check the Delorean's internal systems. He leaned over and searched for the screws he removed, using his hand to brush away layers of dirt and trash from the narrow hallway.

Finally giving up, he sighed, and leaned the panel on the wall, hesitating for a moment to make sure it wouldn't topple over. Using the wall, he pressed his hand to it and got to his feet, his boot clanking loudly on the metal grid floor of the access hallway which ran along the perimeter of the mid-sized freighter.

At one point in its life, the Delorean had been a standard issue transport freighter, just like any other in Federation space, but once Jedidiah Kramer had gotten his hands on it, it had become its own unique thing.

Much of the cargo space had been maintained, that was a necessary element of Jed's smuggling operations, but he'd wired a rudimentary artificial intelligence into the navigation and weapons systems, and had added several other layers of shielding, both physical and energy-based.

Lastly, he'd vastly upgraded the existing onboard defensive systems with quad-barreled hard light blast cannons, integrating them with the onboard AI to provide a layer of automated defensive and offensive capabilities.

The corridor curved gently around and he walked it quickly, soon reaching the front of the ship where there was a wide set of double doors leading to the actual cockpit. Perched at the head of the ship, the cockpit was a broad, rounded snout, a translucent polymer shield wrapped along the curved surface, looking out into the vastness of space.

Lork sat in the co-pilot's chair, a perched, cushioned seat nestled into a console with countless switches, buttons and status screens stretched out before it. Lork twisted his slender neck and looked back at Jed as he entered.

A member of a mammalian race called the Orrakk, he resembled an earthen rodent, most notably, Jed thought, a squirrel, based on the rounded slope of his fur-covered head, lanky form and thick stretch of fur along his spine. He had no tail and walked on two legs instead of four but based on the limited exposure Jed had to species found an earth, he thought squirrel seemed like the most appropriate.

He had a short, but complicated history with Lork, but by and large, was happy to have him as a co-pilot on the ship, even if their tastes and goals weren't so closely aligned.

"What am I looking at, Lork?" Jed asked, sliding himself into the pilot's seat, a chair just like the co-pilot's, but on the port side of the cockpit. The blanket of space spread out before them, pock-marked with a scattering of stars, but there was a soft, blue light slowly glowing in the distance. Lork's long fingers adjusted some controls, and a semi-transparent grid of their section of space overlaid the windscreen before them, tiny identifying marks labelling several of the star systems before them.

Leaning over, Lork pressed his fingers to the soft, blue orb and spread them apart, magnifying that section of space.

"Well, I'll be damned," Jed said, leaning forward to look. There was a tiny line of Federation text labeling the orb.

Federation Outpost 844-X

"That's the place?" Jed asked, looking at Lork. His co-pilot shrugged gently.

"The documents referenced 844-X but made no mention of it being a federation outpost."

"The last report I heard was that the Federation wasn't in possession of the Wilson Sphere," Jed said, quietly.

"And this — Wilson Sphere," Lork replied, "is there a reason why they would want to be in possession of it?"

This time it was Jed's turn to shrug.

"It's supposedly an ancient Earth relic. I can't imagine it holds much value to the Feds, but who the hell knows how they think."

"You were — in their Navy at one point, were you not?"

"We don't talk about that," Jed replied, leaning back slightly and checking the status screens on his console. His fingers adjusted a dial and he tapped at a small keypad, bringing up a narrow screen.

"No signs of life," he said quietly.

"Were you expecting some?"

Jed shook his head. "Not necessarily, but according to that dirt-bag on Juxane, it was a human outpost, at least at some point."

"The Federation label would indicate otherwise."

"The humans and the Feds aren't necessarily besties these days," Jed replied, flicking a switch, then wrapping his fingers around two control sticks attached to the console. "Taking manual control, pre-paring for orbital descent."

The stars around them shifted slightly as the Delorean slowed, then angled, bringing the small, blue orb to the center of the screen covering the cockpit.

"Humanity is new to this solar system," Lork explained, "you can't blame the Federation for being a little—hesitant to accept them into the fold."

"It's not humanity's fault their world was destroyed," Jed said, still looking at the screen as he coaxed the control sticks forward, moving closer to the orb.

"Do we even know the world was destroyed. Those are the ru-mors, but my species has never been especially fond of rumors. We find far more solace in the embrace of the facts."

"We don't all have the luxury of facts," Jed replied. "For some of us, we have no facts to turn to. Just rumor, speculation—"

"And these relics?" Lork asked. "Like the Wilson Sphere?"

Jed nodded. Truth be told, nobody seemed to know exactly what had happened to Earth so long ago. Just that it had been destroyed, its inhabitants scattered to the stars. Their forced exit from their home world had brought them to Federation space, a section of the solar system humanity had not even been aware of prior to their dramatic exfiltration from their home world.

But that was all Jed really knew. And he didn't really know it, he just suspected, based on the conversations he'd had throughout his smuggling career.

Because of their newness and their relatively primitive technology, humankind had been seen as the runts of the Federation, little more than pests, and hadn't even been allowed at the seat of the political table with the other races who ran the interstellar government.

It was a source of much frustration and bitter resentment amongst humanity, a fact that Jed had gleaned from his limited exposure to other humans. Throughout his life, he'd spent far more time with the other races than his own kind, though his intense desire to find out more about his home world had eventually become too much to ignore.

"Approach with caution, Jedidiah Kramer," Lork said quietly. "The artificial atmosphere is still in place, in spite of the lack of life signs. It does appear, at one point, that this outpost was terraformed."

Jed's hands moved over the controls, adjusting the trajectory and angle of the freighter's descent.

"Diverting power to front shields," he said. "Making contact with the upper atmosphere in three — two — one."

The ship jerked and bucked, the control sticks thrashed in Jed's hands, but he held tight, easing them forward and down, and guided the narrow profile of the mid-sized freighter through the turbulent air above the outpost.

After several moments of ship-jarring bucking and jerking, the blunt nose of the ship descended through the lower stretches of atmosphere and into a mustard yellow sky, peppered with dull, gunmetal clouds.

Stretching out beneath them, Jed could see this mysterious destination, the orbital construct known as Outpost 844-X. The surface must have been organic at one point, likely a massive chunk of asteroid that had broken loose and fallen into the nearby planet's orbit. But evidently either the humans or the Federation after them had built over it, encasing much of the surface in layers of plate metal, creating a strange, uneven pattern along the surface of the rock.

"There," Jed said quietly, pointing a finger through the window before them. Among the angled metal texture of the outpost was a larger, almost pyramid-shaped structure, standing above the rest, dark and imposing against the churning clouds behind it.

"It resembles a Federation Citadel," Lork said, leaning forward a bit. His fingers adjusted some of the controls, and he looked down at another status screen. "Besides the terraforming equipment I'm seeing no signs of power to the structure or surrounding perimeter. On the surface, the outpost appears — abandoned."

"Is a Federation outpost ever truly abandoned?" Jed asked, looking into the dark eyes of his fur-covered companion.

Lork clicked his teeth together, his dark nose twitching slightly.

"I suppose, Jedidiah Kramer," he replied, "we are about to find out."

*

Chapter Two

THE WINDS WHIPPED AROUND THE narrow profile of the freighter as Jed guided the ship down towards the metallic surface of the outpost below. Grit and scattered small debris spun up from the ground as Jed activated the slow descent landing thrusters—small, in-wing turbines slowly rotating down and blasting jets of compressed air to the ground to level the landing posture of the ship.

The cockpit was silent as Jed verified the yaw and pitch of the craft, lined up the landing skids, and set the Delorean down with a jolting thud, airlines hissing and the turbine spin slowing by the second, until all was quiet.

"That might very well be your best landing yet, Jedidiah," Lork said, matter-of-factly, his eyes still affixed to the control panel in front of him.

"Was that supposed to be a compliment, furball?" Jed asked and snapped open the clasp of his harness, letting the belt retract into the seat.

Lork's head tilted strangely as he arose on elongated, muscular legs, his booted feet navigating a space designed for smaller species.

"What else would it be?" he asked.

"Good point. I know you're still perfecting the art of sarcasm."

Lork seemed confused by this statement, but let it go, bending over a center status screen that was wedged between the pilot and co-pilot consoles.

"The air outside appears to be breathable," Lork said and Jed looked at the screen to verify that fact. With a tapping of keys, he translated the characters which verified the right percentage of nitrogen, oxygen and other trace elements that would support the typical human respiratory system. Lork's mammalian species also was able to breathe the same air, which was a big reason why the two of them had been able to operate so effectively together.

"Arm up," Jed said, nodding towards a weapons rack next to the co-pilot's chair and Lork obliged, slipping his three long, slender fingers around the body of a rectangular weapon colored in brushed metal with twin, square-ended barrels. Slinging it over one shoulder, Jed retrieved his own energy pistol from beneath the console near the pilot's seat, slipping it into the holster at his hip.

As he holstered his weapon, Lork retrieved another piece of equipment, a scanner of some kind and held it, adjusting a few of the dials and settings with his free hand. There was a soft blip, blip, blip sound as the humanoid rodent glared down at the angular screen in his hand.

Reaching over to the panel on the wall to his left, Jed opened the cover and eased down a red switch. Somewhere beneath them there was the low hissing of hydraulics' and a ramp extended from the belly of the freighter, lowering until it finally clanged against the metal platform beneath them.

"Curious," Lork said as he twisted one of the small dials on the scanner.

"What's that?"

"Besides the terraforming equipment there appears to be no energy signatures and no life forms on this outpost at all. It, by all appearances, is a dead chunk of rock and metal."

"Then this should be nice and easy."

Lork lifted his dark eyes.

"You trust these documents you received? The man providing them seemed barely able to stand upright, he was so imbibed on Scolai Spirits."

"He just gave me the documents," Jed replied, "he didn't write 'em." Reaching into the chest pocket of his long duster, Jed pulled out the folded fabric. Leaning forward, he stretched the thin material over the console, then plucked a small pen light from another pouch on his long coat, shining the light onto the document, which had apparently been written on the leathered flesh of an animal.

There were many characters impossible to translate on the document, but there were several references to 844-X and to the Wilson Sphere, the words written in a language Jed actually understood. Using familiar characters that were rumored to have been sourced on the planet his ancestors lived on.

The planet that had been destroyed so long ago.

"They even identify the sector and the approximate coordinates," Jed said, pointing to another section of text on the document, and comparing it to the navigation screen on the console, which provided similar information. "What's the worst that can happen?"

"Please don't say that," Lork said. "Every time you say that something worse, indeed, does happen."

"Not every time."

"Every time," Lork replied, nodding. "I've counted. I think I have a detailed log here somewhere if you want to—"

"Shut it, rat face," Jed said, folding his document back into a small enough square to slide back into his pocket. Lork shrugged, then nodded, following the human as he made his way from the cockpit and back into the body of the freighter, towards the exit ramp.

*

Chapter Three

JED SHIELDED HIS EYES AS a fierce, whipping wind cut in over the uneven, metal-covered terrain. As Lork had surmised, the air was breathable, but that didn't mean it was pleasant, and there was a persistent, lingering stench throughout the area that they'd landed in. It smelled like grease and rust, like an old, worn down shipyard in desperate need of maintenance.

As they'd noticed upon descent, the sky was a putrid color of swirling, murky yellow, the gray clouds floating within the strange horizon like thick, dark oil mixed with a bowl of urine. Jed's stomach churned slightly at the thought of it as he looked around at the expansive platform where they'd landed.

The Delorean had set down in the shadow of the Federation Citadel, a looming, thick, blocky structure shaped somewhat like a squat pyramid, and at the base of the pyramid was a large, utilitarian statue.

Apparently built of ornate, aged metal, the statue was nearly two meters tall and wider than both Lork and Jed standing shoulder -to-shoulder. Its carved face was impassive, three pairs of deep-set eyes sitting dark in the pale haze. It had six total arms, three perched on each side of its large, bulky torso, and twin legs, thick as the old redwood trees Jed had heard about on planet Earth back in the day.

"The hell is that thing?" Jed asked, looking up at the looming statue which almost seemed to be looking back down at them.

Lork leaned forward, seemingly investigating it.

"I cannot place the source of origin," he said quietly. "I would have thought that perhaps it was left over human artistic expression, but it bears the size of a Luxon, yet the spindly, numerous appendages of the insectile Ketarian."

"Something religious?" Jed asked. "I've heard rumors that these citadels are built as monuments to the celestial overlords that these aliens consider 'God' of a sort."

Lork rubbed the three fingers and one thumb of his fur-covered right hand over his narrow chin, brow knitting as he looked at the construct.

"That much is true, Jedidiah Kramer, but there is nothing of religious significance that I can perceive with this artwork. It looks far more — utilitarian."

"Well, we didn't come here to evaluate art," Jed said, approaching what appeared to be an entry doorway into the citadel structure. He'd slung a canvas sack over one shoulder and as he neared the doors, he slipped it off and set it on the ground.

"Are you sure this is a good idea?" Lork asked. "You believe humans were here at one point — that they designated this as an outpost. Clearly the Federation took issue with that."

Jed looked around them.

"Doesn't look like the Federation has been around for a while." He unlatched his bag and started rummaging through it. "You know it's stuff like this that really chaps my hide," he continued.

"Chaps your — is this one of your Earth colloquialisms again?"

Jed ignored the question.

"I mean, the humans set up an outpost out here, right? Far away from the center of Federation space. Just their own little spot to hang out. So, what do the Feds do? They run them off and take it over, then just leave it to rot. What's the point, huh?"

"I do not truly understand the Federation mindset," Lork replied. "That's partly why you found me in that prison camp. My species — we have an analytical mind and there are things the Federation does that defy analysis. The Orrakk — we do not respond well to that. I, perhaps, respond less well than most."

Jed dug through several items in the bag and finally retrieved a slender, metallic tool. Still in a kneeling posture, he leaned towards the control panel next to the door and pressed gently, sliding it to the right and exposing a computerized locking system behind it.

"Lock is powered," he said. "Without power, we're not getting in."

Lork looked around him, the entire landscape awash in darkness, lit strangely tan beneath the yellowing sky.

"I see no power anywhere," he said.

Jed was already working, accessing some concealed latches on the locking interface. Swapping out one tip of the tool, he replaced it with another, then used the second tool to loosen the clasps of the panel and remove the faceplate of the lock, exposing a network of wires and clamps within the wall of the citadel.

"Let's see what we can do about that," he said quietly, pulling out his light again and shining it into the interior of the wall. "Ahhh," he said quietly, "here we go." Navigating his tool into the dark section behind the wall, he touched a button and a bright light sizzled from within the wall of the citadel. Jed murmured something too low to hear and swapped the tip of his tool out again, then went back to work.

Torqueing his arm as if tightening something, he drew back.

"Got it!"

There was a sudden, low humming noise, the sound of a small engine revving up and Lork took a cautious step backwards. Suddenly, small lights on the console by the locking system flickered to life and Jed quickly replaced the keypad and tightened it down with his tool, smiling as pale green illumination brought the pad to life.

"How — how did you — "

"Pure skill, fur ball, pure ski — "

Jed didn't finish his sentence. Even as the console lit back up and the humming within the citadel wall stopped, more humming emanated from elsewhere on the platform. Lork looked left and right trying to identify the source, then finally took another uncertain step backwards, his dark eyes widening.

"What's your issue?" Jed asked, slipping the tool back into the bag and slinging the bag over his shoulder.

"The humming noise," Lork whispered, "I think it's coming from the statue."

"Say what?" Jed asked, looking at the hulking sculpture, turning his head slightly to listen. There was no doubt about it. A low, building, resonating hum was coming from within the large sculpture, the distinctive sound of gears grinding and an engine spinning up to power.

Lork and Jed looked nervously at each other, then back at the statue just in time for the six dark eyes to wink to luminescent life.

"That's—not a statue is it?" Jed asked.

"I do not believe so, Jedidiah Kramer."

There was a metallic grinding noise and one of the limbs slowly began to lift, caked rust breaking apart, flaking off and spilling to the ground as the arms slowly began to move.

"I suggest we get back to the ship," Lork said quietly.

"Uh uh," Jed replied, shaking his head. He turned to the door of the citadel again and tapped at the keypad. There was another rending, metallic screech and one of the thick legs moved, snapping more rust free of the metallic limb.

Lork was already slipping the double-barreled rifle from his shoulder, moving it in his hands, drawing it close with his long, narrow arms.

"Jedidiah!" Lork said, sounding a little frantic. "What are you doing?"

Jed continued hacking at the keypad.

The large statue paused for a moment, turning as its second foot appeared to be stuck in place. Lork leveled the blaster and fired, twin searing beams of purple light slamming hard into the metal beast's thick torso.

The beams struck and scattered, bursting into a vibrant splash of light before dissipating across the thing's broad torso, leaving no sign of damage.

Its head twisted around, six eyes flashing and it yanked hard, ripping its second leg free, more rusting metal snapping apart as it finally took another lumbering step forward. Its massive foot slammed down on the metal terrain, crashing with an echoing bang and Lork almost fell as he tried to scamper away.

"Jedidiah!" he shouted and leveled the rifle again, firing one more time, and again, the beams striking and deflecting from the construct's metallic hide.

"In!" Jed screamed. "We're in!" He slapped a green, lit button and the doors slipped open, revealing a corridor into the citadel. In a swift sweeping motion, Jed removed the blaster from its holster, held it in two hands, and fired at the approaching sentinel, both shots striking it full in the face, both shots bursting away like fireworks, with no damage done.

"Uh," Jed stammered, "time to go!"

Lork lurched forward, charging through the opened door and Jed slipped in behind him as the robotic thing charged, its legs thudding on the ground as it barreled towards them. Just inside the citadel, Jed whipped around and pounded an emergency button which slammed the entrance door closed, sealing them within.

Just outside, a collision shook the entire structure as the attacking sentinel plowed into the closed door that barricaded Lork and Jed from the dangers outside.

*

Chapter Four

"I THINK YOU MIGHT BE out of your mind," Lork said quietly, as the door shuddered with an echoing boom. "I mean—legitimately insane."

Jed glowered at him as he stood by the wall, looking at what appeared to be a map stuck to it.

"Storage room," Jed said, thrusting a finger at a spot on the first level, near the rear of the structure. "Anything they might have confiscated from the humans who used to be here, they'd likely put it there, right?"

Before Lork could answer, another bone-jarring pound shook the door and Jed saw the metal plate buckle slightly.

"Uh oh."

"Uh oh?" Lork asked, then followed Jed's nervous gaze. "Uh oh," Lork agreed. There was another bang and another dent punched in the metal door.

"What is that thing?" Jed asked.

"If I had to guess," Lork replied, "an old school Federation Sentry. They—don't look like that anymore, but typically in places like this, when they don't want to deploy an actual detachment, they will leave automated defenses."

"You couldn't have maybe given me some of that insight before we landed on this stupid rock?"

"There were no energy signatures," Lork replied. "Everything was fine until you turned the power on, Jedidiah Kramer!"

"Jed, dammit. My name is Jed for the last time!"

Lork drew back.

"There is no reason for hostility. We are both on the same side."

There was another jarring bang and the seam between the double doors split slightly, the thick metal bending inwards.

"Tell that to the crazy robot on the other side!" Jed sputtered.

"I'm not sure that would work," Lork explained. "But I'm willing to try anything—"

The doors shuddered, banged and suddenly blew inward, ripping free of their housing, a huge trio of piston-powered fists ramming through the metal plate and knocking the doors into the entry way.

"Holy shit!" Jed shouted and fired his pistol, sending a half dozen thick beams of bright energy towards the sentry. It ducked its head and drew back slightly, as the first two shots glanced from the wall above it, then it charged again, powered by thick legs and bashed through the wall, smashing thick rock into a dozen ragged chunks, bursting into the citadel with them.

"We need to go, we need to go, we really, really need to go!" Jed stammered as he fired several more beams, Lork joining in with some well-placed rifle fire as well. None of the impacts seemed to affect the sentry at all and it lurched back up to its feet and loomed above them.

"Hallway!" Jed said, reaching out and clamping his hand around Lork's thin arm, then drew him towards him and shoved him into the corridor opposite the front door, both of them stumbling into clumsy running.

"End of this hall! Down the left passage! Storage room! Wilson Sphere!" Jed yelled, glancing over his shoulder.

The sentry filled nearly the entire field of his vision as it drew closer to the hallway opening, seeming to measure it with its six eyes, trying to figure out how to fit its broad form into the narrow passage.

"This Wilson Sphere better be important!" Lork said, looking back the same way that Jed had. The sentry took a step back, as if recalculating its approach, then charged forward again. Too broad to fit through the hallway, instead his massive frame smashed apart the walls as it forced its way through, sending ragged cracks through the structure of the citadel.

"It is — still coming!" Lork exclaimed.

"So I hear! Persistent son of a bitch, ain't he?"

"I do not know what a bitch is," Lork replied, "but I don't believe the sentry is anyone's offspring!"

Jed coughed a ragged laugh in spite of the impending danger, their legs pumping as they sprinted down the hall. Behind them, the noise of smashing walls and metal grinding against hard stone were getting louder by the moment, and he knew by the expression on Lork's face that the sentry was getting closer and closer to catching up to them.

Lork was outpacing him by a considerable margin, his lanky limbs, narrow frame, and animal-like anatomy imbued him with greater-than-human speed and agility. He reached the end of the hallway and spun around, lifting the rifle to his shoulder. Jed angled left slightly, hugging the wall and could almost feel a scattering of small debris peppering his back from the approaching sentry, the cacophony of walls crushing drowning out almost all else.

Twin beams of purple light screamed towards him, then roared past his right shoulder. Heat broiled his neck, and he could feel it all along his back, even through the duster, as the energy beams rebounded off the thick hide of the sentry and splashed into fading light.

"He's getting closer!" Lork shouted and fired again, though Jed knew the second shot would do no better than the first. Jed reached across his body, groping around in the bag as he ran, his lungs hitching with gasping breaths.

The corridor ended about twenty yards ahead and he was approaching fast, but they had to do something. Finally his fingers closed on the contoured grip of what he was searching for.

Beneath his feet, he could feel the floor buckling as the sentry charged forward, its momentum and weight crushing not just the walls, but putting cratered dents in the floor as well.

Jed swept the device from his bag and held it in front of him.

"Use it!" he screamed, and threw it to Lork, who somehow managed to sling his rifle back on his shoulder and catch it in two practiced paws. His eyes scanned the item briefly and quickly realized what Jed had thrown. Nodding, Lork darted right, then swiveled and fired left, shooting a projectile across the hallway, its metal barbed tip burying itself deep in the stone wall across the way.

Jed was almost there. Snapping the secondary barb loose, Lork rammed it hard into the stone wall nearest to him and looked up from where he crouched, nodding at Jed, who nodded back.

Reaching the end of the hallway, Jed leaped, landing less than gracefully in the next corridor which intersected the first. His momentum carried him right, slamming into the hard wall with his shoulder, but he bounced free and leaped forward just as the sentry barreled down after him.

Jed had leaped, and had managed to jump over the taut, titanium grapple line that Lork had strung across the opening at the end of the hallway. The sentry wasn't nearly so nimble.

Its thick ankle struck the taut, strong grapple, a twisted titanium composite designed with a tensile strength of nearly half a ton. The sentry toppled forward, losing its balance, turning to glare at Lork

123

and Jed, its three right shoulders plowing hard into the opposite wall of the intersecting hallway. He collided with a deafening crash and the robotic thing was nearly swallowed by one of the exterior rooms as debris and shattered rock blasted outward from the point of impact.

"Keep going!" screamed Jed.

"That won't stop it!" Lork replied, reaching to his belt and removing a thin, metallic cylinder from a sheath there. "Go! Find your precious artifact!"

"If you die trying to protect me, I'm going to be so damn pissed!" Jed shouted as he ran down the corridor towards the storage room a short distance ahead.

Lork didn't answer. He pressed a release on the cylinder and a glowing shaft of light extended from the hilt, an energy cudgel of sorts. It was a weapon of the Orrakk species, crafted by his ancestors, a thick shaft of powerful metal coated in a layer of kinetic energy. He had little confidence it would stop the sentry, but he had no confidence that the blaster would and little was better than none.

"Come and get me," he said quietly, spinning the cudgel artfully in one hand.

*

Chapter Five

JED SKIDDED TO A HALT outside the open door, his head swiveling to look inside. Stacks of boxes and crates lined the perimeter of the small room on one side, while the other was filled with piles of spilled containers, scattered clothes and other items in haphazard bunches.

Jed looked back down the hallway in time to see the sentry push itself free of the wall, showering more rocks across the floor. Two hands clawed at its head, swiping away dust and debris as it loomed over Lork, glowering down at the slender form of the Orrakk first mate.

Lork moved with a strange, feral grace, instinctively dodging and weaving as the sentry thrashed its arms, slamming hard into each wall as it tried to land a killing blow. Lork slipped beneath one particularly furious strike, then rammed the sentry's skull with his cudgel before back-flipping out of the way of a follow-up strike, landing gracefully two meters away from the metallic automaton.

"Please do not look at me!" Lork shouted, glancing back at Jed. "Find your silly sphere!"

Jed ducked back into the storage room as he heard the muffled thoom of another impact, then began rummaging through the piles of discarded clothes and refuse. It was easy for him to tell that most of these items were indeed of human origin, but of more recent human origin. Items that humankind had built or produced in the far reaches of space, and not items that might have originated on Earth.

Throwing clothes aside and tipping over other containers, he continued to rummage through the items in the small room, his heart hammering with every single shattering bang he heard in the corridor outside.

"Jedidiah Kramer!" Lork shouted. "Now would be good! Apparently, the sentry has arm cannons!"

Jed swiveled his head just in time to see yellow beams of energy scorch the hallway outside, hurtling past and slamming against the rock wall beyond. A moment later, Lork sprang into view, somersaulting, tucking into a tight ball as more fire raced just above him, setting his fur aglow in a soft, off-white refraction of light.

Twisting back onto two legs, knees bent, cudgel still clamped around one hand, Lork twisted and looked at Jed with pleading eyes.

"Hold on, hold on!" Jed shouted and ripped off the cover to another metal container he'd found pressed up against the rear wall of the storage room. Fumbling through the clothes, he could hear Lork's muffled grunts as he jumped and dodged, just trying not to be killed by the lumbering, implacable sentry.

"He's not stopping!" Lork shouted. Jed looked over his shoulder as another beam of energy slammed into the wall to Lork's right, blasting a shower of rocks and catapulting the squirrel-like creature into the storage room with him. A huge, thudding foot crashed hard into the floor as the sentry took a step forward, its massive frame now filling the entire doorway to the room, blocking out all view of the hallway outside.

Jed could see what Lork meant. Four of its six arms were still closed in tight fists, but the upper arm on each side now had rectangular barrels jutting from the wrist where a hand had been, and those barrels drew closer, focusing attention on Jed and Lork.

Wheeling right, Lork grabbed one of the metal containers and hurled it at the sentry as hard as he could, just as the sentry fired. The container exploded, showering them with small, jagged shards of metal, but it had succeeded in offsetting the energy blast and keeping it from frying them where they stood.

"Holy shit I've got it!" Jed screamed, diving down into the final container. He swept an object free of the piles of clothes and slammed it back into the bag slung over his shoulder. "The Wilson Sphere! I found the damned Wilson Sphere!" He patted his bag to indicate his success.

"I am very happy for you," Lork said, pushing himself back so he was shoulder to shoulder with Jed, both of them standing, backs against the real wall of the room.

"Perhaps your God will let you take it into your next life?"

The sentry adjusted its stance, aimed its limb-cannons and for a brief moment, Jed thought he might have actually seen a glimmer of grim satisfaction in the automaton's eyes.

*

"Down! Down!" Jed screamed, wrapping his arm around Lork's shoulders and pushing them both down to the hard floor. Twin energy beams burned the air above them, smashing into the rock wall behind them and blowing a ragged, opened hole through it, pelting rock shrapnel in all directions.

The sentry almost seemed to snarl in anger though Jed couldn't see a mouth on the things mostly featureless skull. Turning and looking over his shoulder, Jed's eyes widened. Apparently, the storage room had been at the rear of the first level of the citadel, and the errant blast had blown a hole out into the night sky beyond.

"We have an exit!" he screamed, slapping Lork hard on the shoulder. The sentry drew back and charged forward, head lowered, its shoulders rammed fissured cracks into the stone wall as it tried to force its way in.

"C'mon!" Jed shouted, hefting Lork up and around, guiding him towards the hole in the rear wall of the structure. Lork slipped free and leaped down onto the metallic terrain, landing in a graceful crouch.

Jed scrambled to his feet, turning, hearing the low hiss of collecting energy. Throwing himself clumsily forward, he sprawled free of the hole just as twin beams of light pierced the sky above him, searing just over his back as he toppled from the blasted hole in the wall and struck the ground with a painful, shoulder-first slam.

"The ship, Jedidiah Kramer. We must get to the ship!" Lork helped Jed to his feet and gestured towards the Delorean which seemed to be an impossibly far distance away. Jed nodded and followed along behind Lork, who was running exceptionally fast, his lanky legs sending him surging at speeds far faster than Jed could ever reach.

Looking back, he noticed that the sentry was not in the storage room they'd just left. In fact, he couldn't see the automaton at all.

That did little to settle the churning in his guts as he ran, his feet jolting over the uneven metal terrain, his lungs burning. Every few strides, he pressed a hand to the bag over his shoulder, just to be sure it was still there.

"Keep running!" he shouted to Lork, as if the alien needed his encouragement. Jed ran harder, slipping his pistol from its holster, just in case, though by all accounts it had almost seemed as though they had slipped away —

The explosion nearly threw him off his feet. A large section of the citadel wall suddenly cracked and burst outward in a cloud of smoke and light. With a metallic screech, the sentry charged from this hole and landed with a jarring thud, hitting the ground so hard it nearly knocked Jed over.

Stumbling, barely regaining his balance, he fired three haphazard shots at the sentry, each beam of hard light pounding harmlessly from the thing's metal skin. The ship was close, but not close enough. Lork had vanished, likely making it inside, but that gave Jed little confidence as the sentry loomed just behind him, its long, powerful strides more than enough to close the distance.

A powerful hand swept up and down, hammering into the ground just behind Jed and he sprawled forward, striking the ground and rolling awkwardly, still too far away from the Delorean to make it to safety.

Rolling over, his eyes widened as the sentry stood tall above him, its massive frame blotting out a wide expanse of mustard colored sky. Coalescing balls of rippling energy formed in the barrels of its arm-cannons, and Jed could almost feel the heat collecting from where he lay.

Inching backwards, he scooched away, trying to put some distance between himself and the metallic giant, but the jointed cannons followed his every move, continuing to recharge and prepare for the killing blow.

There was a sudden flash, a sizzling whine of displaced air, and the familiar searing heat of pulsing energy.

But it was coming from behind him, soaring over him, and plowing headlong into the broad chest of the looming sentry. Four beams of solid light blistered into the large automaton, forcing it backwards, its arm cannons discharging up into the pale sky. Gray clouds swirled around the beams of light as they buried themselves in the heavens.

"Get in!" a familiar voice said and Jed twisted around on his elbows, seeing the Delorean's weapons systems trained on the sentry, its turbines just starting to spin up, kicking dust and dirt in circular waves.

Already the sentry was recovering from the cannon blast, taking another lumbering step forward, but Jed was on his feet and sprinting again. Slowly, the freighter began to take off, the landing skids easing their way off the ground, and Jed had to leap, arms outstretched, fingers barely clawing onto the lip of the ramp.

His arms burned with the pain of holding himself up, the full weight of his body supported by his sharply bent fingertips. Pushing through the pain, he pulled himself up, hand-over-hand, crawling up the ridged texture of the ramp, his heart slowly settling with each passing motion.

Then he saw it. The huge, leaping shape to his right, the sentry had thrown itself into the air, clutching onto the port side landing skid with two of its six limbs.

Immediately, the Delorean pitched to port, listing dangerously, its upward momentum suddenly halted by the additional weight. Wind blistered Jed as he crouched on the downward ramp, cold air biting at him, dirt and grit pelting him from the downdraft of turbines in the Delorean's wings.

The sentry seemed to turn its head and look at him, all six eyes gleaming with a strange artificial hatred. It lifted one more limb, reaching for the ramp, trying to get another handhold, to pull itself up and in.

Jed brought the blaster around in two hands, pushing himself further up the ramp, aiming the weapon, not at the sentry, but at the port side landing skid. He fired twice, striking the joint of the skid, shearing metal and breaking away the bolts that kept the skid attached to the wing's super structure.

The skid jerked, ripped free, then broke loose, tearing away from the wing in a shearing metal screech. Eyes glowing white hot, the sentry fumbled for an additional grasp, but failed, and spilled away, tumbling from the freighter, end-over-end as it went noiselessly through the night air until it crashed down onto the ground a hundred meters below with a satisfying metal-on-metal crunch.

*

The ramp closed, Jed made his way through the access corridor, using his hand to steady himself, trying to swallow his heart back down into his chest.

Lork emerged from the cockpit, looking at him with his wide, dark eyes.

"While I am pleased you are alive, I must question the strategy of removing our landing skid. Eventually, we will need that, will we not?"

"That's a tomorrow problem," Jed gasped. "Let me enjoy this for a minute, would ya?"

Lork shrugged, watching as Jed clawed his way down the hall, sucking in air, using the sleeve of his duster to wipe away the sweat from his forehead. Without a word, he navigated to the pilot's seat and nearly collapsed into it, blasting out one last ragged breath of air. His bag thumped to the floor next to him and he craned his neck to look out of the windscreen as the citadel grew smaller, the freighter rising through the lower atmosphere and preparing for orbital velocity.

"That was — not fun," Lork said flatly.

"No, no it was not."

Lork settled into the co-pilot's seat, quickly adjusting some settings and using the manual controls to guide the nose of the ship towards an exit vector.

"I hope it was — worth it?"

Jed pulled the bag over in front of himself and dug down inside, smiling widely as he closed his fingers around the object he'd nearly died for.

Sitting back in his seat, he pulled out a small, circular object, white in color, though faded by age. There were, what appeared to be twin red stitches encircling the sphere, almost as though they kept it together.

The word Wilson was stenciled into the fabric of it, and Jed hefted it in one hand, smiling crookedly at the feeling of it.

"The Wilson Sphere," he said, satisfaction evident in his voice.

Lork looked over at it curiously.

"And what does it—do?"

Jed scrunched up his face, turning the sphere over in his hand, looking at it closely as he tested the balance and the weight.

"It used to be part of a game," he said, "a game they played on Earth."

"A game?"

Jed nodded.

"We almost died so you could get a—game?"

"It's from Earth," Jed said, showing Lork the item, turning it over, so he could see it.

"Ah," Lork replied, unsure of what else to say.

Jed wasn't sure what to say either. All he knew was the Wilson Sphere was a relic of Earth, the planet his ancestors were from, a planet which no longer existed, though nobody could quite figure out exactly why. In Jed's mind, owning an Earth artifact meant owning a piece of Earth, and that would just have to be enough.

Talionis

Eliot Bishop

Eliot Bishop is an author that we've been nudging and encouraging along since we formed Stories Rule Press. "Talionis" is his first ever story written for publication. It came out much better than I ever imagined it would and I'm honored to include it in Fight or Flight. I love the dialogue and the characters, and his world building is supremely well done.

We're going to see if we can get Eliot to put together a series of books from this universe. I think they'll be spectacular!

If you enjoy "Talionis", you can find out more about Eliot's work at **http://eliotbishop.com/.**

Enjoy "Talionis"! — MP

"Energy can neither be created nor destroyed; rather, it can only be transformed or transferred from one form to another." – Émilie du Châtelet (1706 – 1749)

Chapter One

Location:
Scutum-Centaurus Arm
355.6954
61,567lyFS
'Dark Space' 0.67ly from local system JL48-2022 "Lincoln's Reach"

I woke when I fell hard against the cot.

"Damn it Jive." I yelled at them, without much energy to my cursing.

"Yeah, yeah. Wakey-wakey, Hedge." Jive chirped back, speaking around a plastic stir stick stuck in their teeth.

"Could you, for once, just give me some warning that you are restoring gravity?"

Jive just giggled and continued tapping at the air as they sat in the pilot seat. I grumbled and got out of the crash-cot in the back of the helm. I picked my jacket up off the deck and gave it a sniff before shrugging and throwing it on.

I had a cursory look at the mirror above the vac-sink at the back of the helm. Same messy brown hair, rough stubble, green eyes. I took off my brown leather jacket and quickly changed my blue shirt with the large soycaf stain on the front for a yellow shirt with a soycaf stain near the hip. At least the jacket would cover it.

"Hey, is it there?" I asked Jive as I climbed up next to the chair.

They took the twisted and chewed stir stick out of their mouth and pointed the wet end towards the view screens. The screens flickered to life as they pointed. They showed just the empty void around us.

They put the stir stick back into their thin-lipped mouth and lifted the operator goggles. Their bright neon-purple eyes still caught me by surprise every time I saw them. Pale white skin in contrast and not a single hair on their head. Not even brows or eyelashes. They might have their own personalities and quirks, but I wouldn't ever get used to the look of androids.

"Yeah, Hedge, right there." They had settled into a higher pitched voice today. It sounded like a giddy child. I hated it right away. Way too much cheer before I had my caf.

"I'm only seeing void here. Can you zoom in?"

They nodded in response and flicked one pale finger in a twisting motion.

The view of space in the bottom right of the screens jumped toward us. Black void with white streaks flew over the screens. The image settled on an irregular mass of black that blocked the pinpricks of stars behind it.

"Won't get a better picture than that Hedge. We're still five thousand clicks out. But both transponders register correct. That black squiggly bit in the middle? That is the wreckage of the Allied Sol Corporation Starliner YTK-736 *Rugged Expanse,* melded with the wreckage of the F.F.O.C.S. *First Stone* battlecruiser."

"The tip was good then." I didn't go so far as to sigh, but relief washed through me.

"Yeah Hedge, it's good news. Better news, I'm not picking up any other transponders within half a light year. We should be alone for a good while."

"Good, glad to hear it. Thanks Jive." With a pat on their shoulder, I turned to leave.

"Yep yep. Hey, do you know what the First Fleet of the Origin Church of Sol was doing out this far? Or why they wrapped their ship around a Corps Fleet transport?" Jive asked.

I didn't turn back as I answered.

"Nah. And I don't really care. We're here for salvage, not to investigate. Get in, get out, get paid. Let's keep this tight. Did you wake the crew?"

"I'm'a guess the grav-kick did that for me!" Jive giggled manically and slipped the operator goggles back down over their eyes. I just shook my head as I left through the back hatch toward the galley.

My ship, *Strix*. She wasn't much to look at. And I liked it that way. Less attention, the better. Mid-sized hauler, nothing too big and not small enough to get tossed in the wash. Perfect for just slipping by in the void while no one's paying attention. *Strix* has been mine for almost six years. She's my one constant. Well, her and Jive. Even though Jive changes their voice every time they cycle. They were both reliable. The crew had changed a few times, some for good reasons, some for bad.

Peeps was the first I saw. He already had the soycaf warming up and just nodded at me as I came close. "Cap."

"Peeps." I printed a second cup and placed it next to his on the counter.

"Can you get the droid to stop grav-kickin us awake one of these days?"

"You've got a better chance than I do. They like you."

"If that's another crack at my ocular implants makin me half robot Cap…" Peeps voice got low as he grumbled at me. He even squinted a little.

"You'll do what? Squint harder at me?" I smirked and waved at him as I walked away. "Ping me when it's hot. I'm gonna go square up the gear."

Peeps' reply was lost as Dang stormed past me, yelling toward the helm. "I will frag you're processors and deep-fry your memory chips as snacks while I watch your tin-can moth-"

"Whoa, whoa, Dang! Reel it back." I placed my hand on her shoulder. "You just need some caf. Calm down, get a drink, have some food. You're worse than a planet-diver after a jump, you know that?"

She just stared me down and shoved my hand off her shoulder. She slumped in a barstool at the galley table, grumbled under her breath while she held her head propped up on both her hands.

Peeps printed a third cup for Dang as the soycaf continued to steam in the pot.

I got to Fawn's quarters and knocked on the bulkhead next to the door. "Hey, rookie, you up yet?"

A dozen seconds later, there was a clatter from inside and the hasty shuffling of cloth.

The hatch sprung open with a pneumatic hiss and Fawn's blonde hair was all I could see. He parted it and raked it back with his fingers. Blonde hair, blue eyes, pale white skin, and skinny. Regular spacer kid. His crooked nose was even sporting a big ugly red pimple. Kid was still young enough to deal with pimples. That'll make ya feel old.

"Yes Captain! I'm up."

"Did I wake you, rookie?"

"I...uh, yes sir."

"The gravity kicking on didn't do that for ya?"

"Uh...no sir. I strap in when I go down. It's...ah, I thought it was sta...doesn't everybody?"

"You read that in a manual somewhere? None of my crew strap in for naps. What would they have to relieve the boredom of space if they didn't have something to bitch about when they woke?" I grinned, but the kid looked concerned.

"So...I shouldn't strap in?"

"Shit, do what you like. Just be sure you're ready for crash and catch in thirty, got it?"

"Yes sir, will do!" He snapped an honest salute at me. I just shook my head.

"Kid, this isn't the Corps Fleet or the O.C.S. Don't salute me."

He slowly lowered his hand and looked abashed like only the young can properly pull off without looking like try-hards.

"Look, your aunt wanted you to get some proper experience and I needed a mechanic. I don't care if you attended the Galactic Scouts' meetings every week before this or what you do after you leave my ship. You're here for six months. Temp only. But while you're on my ship, cut out the sir's and salutes, got it?"

"Yes si...Cap...Hedge?"

"Cap's fine."

"Yes, Cap. Can do." I saw his hand twitch for another salute, but he turned the motion into scratching his bare chest before it reached his forehead.

I grinned at him. "Good. Now go get dressed, fed and caf'd up. We start burning hull in thirty."

*

Chapter Two

Thirty minutes later aboard the F.F.O.C.S. 'First Stone'

THE INTERIOR AIRLOCK DOOR BEHIND us sealed shut. The ring of red around the door flashed green twice and then emitted a soft blue light. Peeps, Dang, the rookie and I all had a look around. Random debris and shorn metal floated in zero-g. No bodies, but there were bound to be some around.

Peeps eyes flashed for a moment before he gave us a thumbs up. Dang was the first to disengage her helmet. As the nanotube filaments of her helmet retracted into her suit, her bright green hair floated out freely in the air. That hair was the same shade as her eyes, and both sharply contrasted with her dark grey nanite-augmented skin. She took a deep snort of air and choked.

"It's rank in here Cap, like burnt bacon. And stale. Breathable, but the recyclers haven't run since the crash. We're breathing dead air."

I disengaged my own helmet as Peeps and Fawn did the same. The smell of stale air hit me first, then the harsh bite of ozone. "You smell that Peeps?"

"Yeah, someone was discharging plasma in here." Peeps walked over to a terminal. He held his palm close to it and a small tether slithered out of his wrist, merging into the terminal. "Just a minute, Cap."

"Get me schematics, cargo manifest, the works."

Peeps nodded. He'd been part of my crew for almost four years, he knew what I wanted by now. His light grey eyes flashed again as reems of information flew through his shaved head. His scraggly red beard clashed with his dark black skin in ways that only stood to highlight his flashing eyes.

"What was that about plasma?" Fawn said in a small voice. "I thought the accords only allowed for ceramic ammunition or hard-light weapons on ships?"

Dang shook her head at him and pulled up her rifle, securing the area. I pulled my own pistol up as I looked back at Fawn. "No matter what the United Galactic Nations put in those accords, you're always gonna have someone breaking them. And a plasma rifle is a hell of a 'Fuck Off' statement when leveled at another being. Most people only abide because otherwise all boarding actions would result in sudden decompression and death for everyone involved."

"But... how do you know that it's plasma from the smell?" He looked baffled as he took a few sniffs.

"Ozone. O-three I think? It's a byproduct of plasma. Something about the heat or electricity or something from the plasma travelling through the air creates ozone, which has a distinct smell. Also," I pointed towards a long scorch mark that Dang had just revealed with her flashlight. "that scoring on the bulkhead and deck is another big giveaway."

"Oh. Right. Ok, so what happened here?"

I just shrugged at him. "Who cares? We're here to retrieve the lightest and most valuable cargo we can and get out quick as current."

"Right, yeah. But...ships don't just crash. Not in space."

"Well that's easy. The OCS ship hit the Corps ship. Corps ship is the one snapped in half and wrapped around this beast. As to why, again—who cares?"

"Sure, I guess. I just…it doesn't make any sense is all. The Corporation and Origin Church aren't currently fighting."

"Look—the Galaxy ain't black and white. There are shades of grey everywhere. And while the Corps and OCS are both big, imposing organizations, they are still just people. OCS is counting converts in the trillions. That's trillions of individuals who all have independent thoughts and feelings. And this ship?" I waved a hand at the dead lump all around us. "This was a tiny fraction of that organization. Less than nine hundred beings at maximum capacity. All guided by one person, the captain—"

"Actually Cap," Peeps interrupted. "The OCS has Archbishop-Marshal's as their top brass on these Archangel-Class Battlecruisers."

"Like I care. Anyways, the point being, it is all run by one being. They get an idea in their head like 'I'm gonna crash this ship into that one.' and they do it. Laws won't hold back someone whose sixty thousand light years from their headquarters."

"Ok…" Fawn nodded along as I spoke. "But…why?"

"We aren't investigators. Leave the 'whys' to the authorities who will eventually show up. I got a tip from a source of mine, we got here first, and we need to leave ASAP with a heavy haul of loot. That's the only concerns that should be on your mind. Peeps, how we comin?"

"Almost there, Cap." Peeps' eyes were closed as he interfaced with the ships computer. "Engine got drained recently, but good news is the energy capacitors are still functioning. They are maintaining emergency power, hence the airlock still working. But the oxygen recycler got slagged at some point in the crash. With all these leaks from hull damage, we'll have somewhere between thirty to forty-five minutes of air. Maybe. They also have a VI in the system, but it's only putting up a tiny bit of resistance."

"Just be glad the OCS has an attitude about AI." Dang chirped at him. "Else you'd be fried soon as you touched the source code."

"And that's why I prefer the jobs where we salvage the OCS. No one tell Jive I said it, but a full-blown AI ain't nothing to mess with. I prefer computer intelligence limited and shackled." Peeps shivered dramatically.

"Explains your choice of shore leave flings." Dang laughed at her own joke and continued to cackle as she explored farther down the hall.

Peeps just shook his head as she left. "She's just jealous that I find flings and she finds—here we go, got it." He disconnected from the terminal and quickly ran through the manifests. "Yep, they got some…a lot of it actually. Looks like they had it strapped and padded as they should. Some of those holes we saw from the outside were auxiliary storage, but the main hold has an independent grav-repulsor system, so the cargo should be intact…all hundred thousand liters of it!" Peeps looked up excited.

I whistle long and low. "That is an awful lot. We could probably take on maybe half that. That's a hell of a haul, nice find."

"Sorry, but a hundred thousand liters of what?" Fawn interrupted.

"Liquid gold, kid." Peeps smiled.

"It's fuel. The stuff that makes us go when we aren't jumping be-tween spiral arms. Liquid hydrogen. The lightest and most valuable resource you can find on any cruiser out here. And we just found a motherload of the stuff." My smile was ear to ear as I turned back to Peeps. "Lead the way, Peeps!"

"Absolutely! Hey Dang! We're moving out!"

Chapter Three

Twenty minutes later, Deck 4, three hundred meters from the hatch into main cargo hold.

I PINGED MY COMM BACK to the ship. "Jive, track my position and find the cargo bay loading door close to us. We'll get it open and secure the cargo from there."

"Yep yep." Jive acknowledged and left the channel.

"Peeps, what gives? I thought you said the capacitors were still providing power?"

"Yeah, they are, but just emergency power. Gotta pry these interior doors open. Gonna be a little slower getting to the hold, but we'll get there." Peeps interjected his reply with grunts as he and Dang pried at the door with crowbars.

Fawn was gulping breaths as we both waited for the door. His hands shook on the shotgun. He coughed a few times and I could see sweat beaded on his forehead. Walking over, I activated his helmet. The orange hardlight bubble popped up immediately. Nanotubes stretched up to quickly form the proper helmet underneath. Once the hardlight popped off again, he's was back to breathing regularly.

"It's just stale air. You get used to it. But don't suffer just to be brave or some shit. You got at least an hour of good air left in the EVS." I could feel my toes starting to tingle. I didn't have much longer before I was gonna be gulping too. "We'll be out of here in less than ten once we hit the hold."

Fawn just nodded at me as he slowed his breathing and consciously calmed his shakes.

I nodded back and deployed my own helmet. The hardlight bubble popped off when the doors sprung open. There was a sucking sound. Trash flew past the doorway, quickly flying out the smooth four-foot diameter gash in the starboard side of the newly revealed hall.

Peeps swore loudly and engaged his own helmet.

Fawn flew passed the doorway before I could register.

Peeps reached for the kid but couldn't catch him.

Dang was faster. She had been reaching for the helmet engage on her wristpad. Instead she disengaged her grav-boots. She pulled at the doorway for extra speed and sailed toward the kid. With one arm outstretched towards Fawn, she blind-fired her rifle back towards Peeps and I. One of several small tubes crowding the bottom of her rifle barrel sparked and burst. A self-propelled rocket the size of a battery shot out of it towards my face.

My first thought was that she'd lost it. In the panic of the moment, she'd hit the wrong button on her rifle and doomed me to a hot and messy end.

I pondered why the propulsion stream behind the tiny missile was black before it made a sudden dive and buried itself deep into the deck. Less than a foot from my toes. The 'propulsion' stream snapped taught into a sharp black line and it clicked into place for me.

Dang had a grip on Fawn's harness as they both dangled in the void like fish on her tether line. Peeps and I walked over to the hole in the hull and reeled them in. Once inside, Dang engaged her boots and helmet before clapping the rookie in the back of the helmet.

"You stupid planet-coddled fuck! Why in the cursed void would you not have your boots engaged!? Did you wanna take a spacewalk? Did I stop a suicide attempt? Or are you really that stupid? Fuckin tourists!" Dang tried to punctuate her statement with another slap but Peeps stepped between them. She seethed and cursed again as she walked back to where her tether had buried itself and busied herself recovering it.

I just shook my head and hauled the kid back to standing. He floated next to me for a moment. His nose was bleeding, the blood smeared inside his visor. Dang's hit had bounced his nose off his visor.

I spun him round so I could reach his wristpad on his left and engaged his boots. His feet shot down a few inches to the deck, jostling more blood from his nose. Another button and his suit engaged a quick vacuum inside his helmet, sucking out the blood from his vision.

He was dazed as he turned his blood streaked gaze toward me.

"You alright kid?"

"She... she saved me. Then tried to kill me." His voice was low and shaky.

I hit another series of controls on his wristpad. The visor flashed orange as the blood was cleared from it. He took a sharp breath as the suit injected a concoction to bring him back to reality. His eyes cleared and he focused on me. I pressed my visor against his and disengaged my comms.

"With her mods, if she'd wanted to kill you, she would have. That dermal nanite shit doesn't just harden the skin." I had to almost shout, but I can tell that my voice vibrations were getting across from my helmet to his. "What were you thinkin? We're on a floating derelict, you always gotta assume the worst." He looked properly abashed as he tapped off his own comms.

"Sorry Cap. I wasn't thinkin. And I've...never done this sorta thing before."

"Your aunt told me you had experience with frigate repair.

146

It's most of the reason you're here kid, I needed a mechanic. If Peeps can't hack it, I need a greaser who can jimmy the tech with his hands."

"I can do that, promise! Cept... I only ever worked on ships in dry-dock. Never went out on call."

I backed away and shook my head. Of course. That's why the kid was here now. His aunt had suckered me into getting him void experience. No one would have ever given the kid a chance on a job if they had to hold his hand during void procedures.

I clicked my comms back on. "Okay kid, you're gonna learn by doing, then. And if you endanger my crew again before we get off this wreck, I'm'a drop you at the next port we come across and you can make your own way back to system, got it?"

Fawn nodded quickly and stood a little straighter. He engaged the vacuum again to clear the new blood, but the flow was slowing.

"Good. Secure your weapon, eyes up, and stay between me and Peeps. Dang, take point. Let's get this H-two and get out ASAP. No more screw ups, got it?" I heard a pair of quick chirps in my comm as Dang signaled positive and moved up without a word. Peeps raised his wristpad and tapped for another positive notification.

With his implants, he didn't need to manually interact with his EVS like that. But he had done it in clear view of Fawn, who imitated the motion after a moment. I wondered if the kid would clue in on the assist. Maybe later, when he'd thought this all through. Fawn fell in step behind Peeps and we all headed to the cargo bay doors.

Chapter Four

THE KID KNEW MECHANICS AT least. Emergency power hadn't extended to the cargo bay hatch and no amount of prying was gonna open a hundred centimeters of dead-locked titanium door. Fawn's plasma torch lit the hall in fitful spurts as Peeps, Dang, and I stood with our back to him.

"Kid owes me a grapple round." Dang was still fuming, but she'd had the forethought to open a private channel before griping about him.

"Yeah I know. Take it up with him after we're off this thing. I need him focused, not shitting himself about an ex-P.O.I. trooper coming after him."

"You said 'learn by doing' before. Is this his first void walk?"

"Just stay on mission Dang. We'll talk things over later." Dang just shook her head and cut the private channel. I sighed and reengaged the broad comm. "How's it comin?"

"Almost through Cap. 'Nother minute to reverse the lock and then we're in." He sounded more confident than I had heard him before. He was in his element, doing something he was good at. At least he had that.

A high-pitched whine screamed through the comms and I jerked my head violently as my body tried to pull my ear away from the sound. It was over as quick as it started, but I saw Dang scan the hall with her rifle, eyes wide.

"What in the cold void was that?" Peeps swore into the comms as he aimed his pistol wildly around the hall.

"Stop with the waving guns people! Damn it. Fawn, was that

you?"

"No sir, Cap. I'm two hands deep into this lock, couldn't have been me." Fawn answered.

"Dang, Peeps? You got something causing feedback?"

"No Cap." Peeps replied as Dang shook her head at the same time. I looked over at Peeps as he holstered his pistol.

"Peeps, find out what the fuck that was." He nodded and relaxed his body. He started to waiver slightly as he focused, searching the signals around us.

"Jive, did you get any feedback on the comms just now?"

"Nah, nothin on my end." They giggled as they answered. "Did I see the new guy trying to greet the void earlier?"

"Not now Jive. Just tell me you're at the loading port." I grumbled.

"I'm at the loading port, Hedge." They had a tinge of glee in their voice as they said it.

"Are you actually at the loading port?"

"Not yet, but I will be soon enough." They giggled again. I sighed heavily and just signaled a confirmation back.

"Cap, you gotta figure out that 'literal command' thing one day." I could hear the grin in Dang's voice as she said it.

"Yeah, yeah, laugh it up stiff-skin. They make those things so life-like I forget sometimes."

"Remember when you told them to take a void walk? That's twelve hours of void combing for a floating android I'd like back." Dang hadn't held back her laughter, but it sounded a bit forced. She'd kept her rifle trained down the hall as she spoke.

"Or how about the time—,"my reply got cut off as the 'channel open' chime dinged into the comms and a stranger had started to speak on our channel.

"Hello!? Are you here to help?" A man's voice, low and quiet like he was whispering into his comm.

Fuck. Just what we needed, a survivor. Dang turned to look at me and I slashed my hand across my throat in a signal not to say shit and repeated the signal for Peeps. He nodded and made an explosion sign with his hand next to his ear and then shrugged as if to say no idea where that feedback came from. I pointed at my ear and mimed fishing and reeling. He gave me a thumbs up and started to trace the new signal from the whispering man.

"I heard you earlier on the ship. I know you are headed to the cargo hold. Are you here to help? Is this the right channel?" The whispering man spoke again.

"We're... ah, we were just passing through and saw the wreck. Figured we'd come check for survivors." Fawn answered.

It was my turn to slap the back of his helmet. I hoped I busted up his nose again. He turned back to me—not bleeding, damn it—and shook his head in a universal What the hell? I just shook my head and hopped on the comm.

"This is Captain Hedge." I put on my best concerned-citizen voice. "As my crewmen said, we noticed the wreckage and headed in for a courtesy check, as per the accords."

"You are illegal salvage, Captain Hedge, no need to lie. Why else would you head directly for main cargo?" the whispering man came back. He sounded indignant.

"That's a serious accusation sir. I would never engage in theft of O.C.S. property or any other and the fact that you would—"

"Captain Hedge." The man interrupted. "I do not care, and we have no time. You must get me out of here and then we need to leave as soon as possible."

I shook my head and looked to Peeps. He shook his head. He can't trace the signal. Dang shook her head at the man's words and I knew she had no qualms about leaving a stranger to the void if it meant one less witness. I looked down at Fawn who was staring up at me and motioned him back towards the door with a wave.

"Ok mystery man. Say we are illegal salvage. If we were, why would we want to save a potential witness? You've got nothing but dead air left in this ship, and not much of it. It'll be at least a few hours before any official repo teams make it out to this stretch of void. Dead men can't spread nasty rumors about what me and my crew may or may not be involved in."

"I can offer you three times the credits that those H-two barrels in main cargo are worth. Half up front, soon as we're on your ship." He came back still whispering, but he hadn't sounded like he was lying. Still…

"Never met a holy man who believed in personal wealth."

"I'm a consultant. I was brought in to…interview a heretic." The man came back, and I swallowed hard.

A consultant brought in to interview a heretic. It was an awfully long way of saying Inquisitor. They were a branch of the Eternal Guard of Tartarus, a now-defunct church who had specialized in information extraction. Generally, by way of torture, and almost always resulting in body disposal.

If the Origin Church of Sol had hired an Inquisitor, there had to have been serious credits involved. O.C.S. had been the destroyers of the Eternal Guard in the first place. No Inquisitor would work for them without a down payment that could purchase a fleet. And even then, most Inquisitors would refuse.

If this Inquisitor was offering cash, and had already accepted a job from the O.C.S., then we could at least trust that he wanted to get tangled up in the law as much as we did. And the one thing you could trust about an Inquisitor was their word. If they said they would do something, they would do it come hell or void between them and their goal.

I looked at Peeps and he shrugged. He was here for the credits, and he trusted my judgement. He'd do what I decided. Dang shook her head slowly, not fully decided it seemed.

"Ok then, Inquisitor. Before we decide, tell us what happened here."

"There is little time." He didn't deny the title. And he sounded tense now, still whispering. "Please. I am inside an escape pod that did not fire on the starboard side of deck seventeen."

Please?

Inquisitors didn't request, they demanded. If I didn't know better, I'd say he was spooked.

"If it will motivate you, send me your personal code and I will transfer a down payment to you right now." My visor lit up as a small code displayed on it from the comm channel. I assumed it was his own code. I replied with mine and waited.

Dang was shaking her head more emphatically. She had decided this was a bad idea it seemed. I muted myself and pushed my visor against Peeps.

"How far is this pod from us?" I asked him.

"Not too far, but the capacitors are almost out. We only have ten more minutes of power on this wreck, max. And we'll use almost all of that getting to his pod. If we pull him out and manually eject the pod, Jive can probably pick us up from there. But I don't want to be here when the safeties on the engine power off."

Uncontained energy from the hard-light drive would rip both these wrecks into pieces. I swallowed. Yeah, nether did I.

"Is there a shorter or faster path?"

152

"We could void walk the exterior. We'd make it to the pod in less than a minute, but we'd have to cut our way inside. I can't hack a pod from the exterior. Still, we'd probably be inside and back on our ship a few minutes faster."

My visor lit up again with a notification. The Inquisitor had sent a down payment. Peeps spied the notification and gasped.

"Cap... that's more than we made in the last three hauls..."

"I am very aware of that Peeps. Now shut you're gaping mouth." I backed away and un-muted my comm. "Ok, seems the credits are real. We'll come get you. Tell me you're suited up."

"Yes, Captain Hedge. I have acquired an emergency EVS from the pod. Please hurry." He whispered back to me and then cut the comm. As soon as he did, Dang was in my ear.

"What in the frozen void are you thinkin, Cap?"

"I'm thinkin we can take a year off with his down payment and maybe a decade if he's paying full retail for a triple value of that cargo hold. Black market would only pay us a third the value and we wouldn't be able to haul half that hold. Getting paid eighteen to one is a no-brainer, Dang."

"He sounds scared." This from Fawn, who had removed his hands from the innards of the door and packed away his tools into his pouches.

"Yeah, he does." Peeps chimed in. "And if an Inquisitor is scared of something, we should all be shitting ourselves."

"Peeps is right." Dang agreed. "We should scrap this whole job. The H-two, the Inquisitor, all of it. Just jump and bail. This whole SNAFU is about to go FUBAR."

"Hey!" I yelled over their voices, a little louder than I had meant to. The three of them jerked their heads at the sound. "This is not a democracy. My ship, my crew, my decision. I've heard you all and that's the end of it. Peeps," I pointed at him. "get us void-side of the hull ASAP. Fawn," I grabbed his wrist and held up the wrist pad to his visor. "Review you're grav-boot and maneuvering thruster controls before we put our bare backs to the frozen void. And Dang..." I trailed off as I looked to her. "just be ready for anything."

They all nodded as I gave my instructions and Peeps started to move down the hall and back towards the smooth hole in the hull that Fawn had almost left from.

*

Chapter Five

"CAPTAIN HEDGE." MY COMM CLICKED at me. It was the Inquisitor's whisper again. "You must hurry. Things are accelerating."

"Yeah, we're goin fast as we can. You failed to mention what you are so worried about."

My crew and I continued our measured pace across the hull of the ship. Above us—at least from our perspective—was the dark void. We clung to the side of the derelict cruisier like fleas to a dog and hoped it didn't try to shake us off.

"As I said, I was commissioned to interview a heretic prisoner. A scientist by the name of Doctor Finis. I am known to have a certain specialty with scientists. It is my niche; I know how they think." Despite the whisper and obvious fear in his voice, he sounded confident in himself.

"I don't need a play by play of your interrogation. Why're you shitting yourself in a lifeless escape pod?" I interrupted.

"You have the time. And you need to understand." He had lost the fear in his tone. Now it was a cool and informative voice.

Maybe I shouldn't piss off an Inquisitor.

"As I was saying, I was specifically requested for my previous successes with this particular brand of heretic. Doctor Finis had been studying Châtelet-Einstein Mass Conversion drive technology. You would know it as your CE-MC drive. Or perhaps just as a hard-light drive."

I nodded along and then stopped when I realized I was on comms. "Yeah, I know what a hard-light drive is. Uses a hard-light field all around a ship to convert mass buildup into energy. I don't know the science, but I know that hitting or breaking lightspeed is impossible without it."

"You are correct Captain Hedge, that is how it works, and really all you need to get by in everyday life. Doctor Finis was intrigued by the scientific theory itself. Simply, let us say this: If you move faster than light, your ship will gather infinite mass just by virtue of its speed or energy. The hard-light field you mentioned absorbs that, converting the mass into energy and shunting it back into the drive. That loop allows us as a species to reach out to any distance we want across the universe in moments as an infinite supply of fuel and speed is created just by the virtue of travelling at that speed."

"Ok, so this Doctor was intrigued by a theory we proved hundreds of years ago?" I had tried to keep up, but none of this was making much sense.

"No, he was more interested in creating a micro-version of that same technology. Doctor Finis theorized that if he could have the body convert mass and energy in the same way at the genetic level, he could end human degradation and essentially provide humanity with its next major step: immortality. A body that never aged, never shut down from use. New energy poured into whatever organ needed it. Injuries recovered from in moments by the body itself rapidly replicating tissue and blood and the host needing only a large meal.

He even went so far as to think he could remove the need for food from the human body, needing only electricity or sunlight to survive."

The Inquisitor sounded impressed, I think. Maybe even excited.

"That all sounds like some fantasy-fringe-science to me. He wanted to put hard-light fields inside humans?"

"I cannot hope to explain it all to you over comm, but I assure you the science was quite sound. Doctor Finis is a true visionary." Yep, he was definitely impressed.

"I can hear the 'but' coming."

His tone was annoyed, but he was no longer whispering as he relayed his story.

"Yes. Well. Doctor Finis was in his eighties when he had this breakthrough idea. He had been working on it for over a decade. He was certain he would not have a clear enough proof with evidence for the accords to allow him to start clinical trials for another few years. And it would be longer than that to administer a safe dose of his experiment to himself, which was his end goal, of course.

"Despite our medical advances, there is a slim chance he would live long enough to enjoy the fruits of his labors. Then he got the news that he had cancer. He became desperate. He moved up his timeline and contacted the V.I.S. drug cartel. They agreed to fund him and hide him as he began clinical trials immediately, outside of the accords."

"Look," I cut in. "It's a dramatic story and all, but what's the end point here?"

The Inquisitor sighed heavily and paused before speaking.

"After six months, the cartel demanded the results he had promised. Without further details, I will say that he dosed himself. And it worked."

"You're saying you interviewed an immortal?"

"Immortal in theory, yes. But the dosing was an experiment. He had not accounted for all the factors. Specifically, his own cancer. You see-"

The hull underneath us suddenly shuddered and bulged.

*

Chapter Six

A HOLE BURST OPEN TEN feet in front of us. White light brighter than a sun lasered through the reinforced titanium like a finger through sand. It had only lasted for a breath. It left behind a smoking red-hot gash, four-foot-wide and almost eighteen feet long. It was exactly the same hole we had almost lost the rookie through in the hall.

"Holy shit! Holy shit! Cap! What da fuck was that?" Fawn screamed as he swung his shotgun back and forth.

Dang held her rifle steady as she waited for the automated UV screen on her visor to clear. She slowly approached the rend in the hull.

I moved towards it and motioned Peeps over. "Tell me what you see Peeps. Inquisitor?"

"I am still here Captain Hedge." He was back to whispering now.

"I don't suppose you were about to tell me that his cancer gave him laser beams coming out of his eyes?"

"Not technically laser beams. And no, not his eyes." It was hard to tell with his whispers, but it sounded like wry amusement in the statement.

"Cap." Peeps motioned me closer. "This is deep. Multiple decks deep. I can't see it all, but I'd guess that came from the engine bay.

"That is him." The Inquisitor answered. "His injection accelerated his cancer while simultaneously consuming his excess growths. He is releasing energy at intervals, and they are speeding up."

"Is he in control?" I whispered, too.

"He threw his last release into the *First Stone's* CE-MC drive. They had just responded to an SOS from the *Rugged Expanse* and were on an intercept course when he burned through his cell hatch, escaped to the engine bay, and overloaded their drive. It converted as it should, but helm could not slow down to a stop before we collided with the *Rugged Expanse*."

"So… actual laser beams. This guy literally shoots laser beams?" Dang's voice cracked.

"It is actually an ionized particle beam of…" The Inquisitor took a brief pause. "Yes. Laser beams."

"I gotta get me some of that juice..." Dang said under her breath, but it still came through on the comm.

"Dang, focus." I hadn't yelled, but I'd made it as firm as possible in a whisper. "Do you have another tether round? We need to cross this gap."

"Yes'ir!" She snapped a mock salute at me and fired across the gap. Peeps took an end and pushed Fawn to go across.

The Inquisitor spoke up. "As his interviewer, I did not want to be seen or heard by him after he escaped. His escape and release into the drive were voluntary expulsions, but he has unwillingly released before. And as I said, they are becoming more frequent. That is all to say, you must hurry, Captain Hedge. I listened via comm as he methodically eliminated everyone on the ship."

"So that explains the scoring and ozone smell. And the hole in the hallway." I had another thought. "But we haven't seen any bodies, what happened to them?"

"He is a living CE-MC drive at this point. What do you think happened to the bodies?"

I could taste bile in my throat. I pushed it down through sheer will.

"Right. Ok. We're hurrying. Triple time folks, let's go."

I stepped forward and held tight to the wire thin cord. It was only four foot across, but that was enough. None of us could have stepped across. Without gravity, hopping was not an option.

I disengaged my boots and pulled myself across. Fawn and Dang both pulled me back to the hull and I reengaged my boots. My right clicked onto the hull. My left almost landed when the hull bucked again.

I felt the heat behind me through my EVS. I saw the beam's light reflected in Fawn's and Dang's visors. It came and went before I had turned to see.

The tether floated toward me, a frayed line. The spot where Peeps had been standing was a red-hot smoldering hole in the hull. Peeps was gone.

*

Chapter Seven

WITHOUT MOVING MY FEET, I turned and reached out for Fawn's left arm. I choked on more bile. I punched in his boot command and he slowly floated away from the hull. I turned and Dang was already floating a few inches away. I disengaged my own and drifted from the ship.

"No no no no no…" Fawn was shaking as his body slowly did cartwheels. His shotgun waving around behind him from the strap on his harness.

"Get it together. We have no time to fall apart. Engage your EVS thrusters now." I was harsh, but I had hoped it would cut through his shock. "If you don't, you'll float off till your air runs out. Or something worse."

Dang clipped her rifle to her side and adjusted her thruster controls. They were old tech, manual only, but they worked fine.

At least our boots where no longer making noisy targets for the unstable doctor inside the wreck.

"Jive. We're just above deck seventeen on the starboard side. Come pick us up." Dang came over the comm sounding much calmer than I would be capable of.

I took a deep breath. "Jive, belay that. Put the wreck of the *Rugged Expanse* between you and the *First Stone* and await further instruction."

The breath hadn't helped, my voice waivered.

"Are you fucking kidding me? Peeps just got vaporized, we can't stay here another second!" She had been screaming into the comms and her voice had cracked at the end. She was terrified. This wasn't something she could hide from or shoot at.

I had felt that fear too.

"We've already taken the money, Dang. And I'm not gonna have another death on my head. Now stop shouting and get moving. We need to get to the pod, disengage it from the ship and release the Inquisitor. And we need to do it real quiet-like."

"Fuck! Fuck. Fine." Engaging her thrusters, she aimed towards the escape pod.

I got to the spinning rookie and straightened him out. "Ok, have you used maneuvering thrusters before?"

"Peeps...he's...he's gone." Fawn was rambling.

"Yes. He is. And we will be too if you don't get your shit locked down. Clip your gun, engage your thruster controls." It was easier to snap a stiff, commanding tone now. When someone else is losing their shit, you either break or harden and help them.

"Right. Ok." Fawn clipped his barrel to his harness. I reached over and engaged his thruster controls and watched as his body became rigid.

"Just like a mining pod. Speed on the left, direction on the right. Think of your suit like a pilot chair. You're just having a seat and steering."

"Right. Yeah, it's like a game I play."

"Good. You'll be a natural, then. Listen, the pod is less than twenty meters that way." I pointed for him. "Just gotta get there and then release the pod. We were gonna cut in and take the Inquisitor out from there. That's not an option anymore. Any chance you know of a *silent* way to eject the pod manually from the outside?"

"Of course. There is a maintenance ejection override, but it's usually engaged by an external rig in drydock." He made it sound like it was the most obvious, simple thing.

"Wish you had mentioned that earlier. Ok, can you override that?"

"I think… yeah, I think I could pull a regulator fuse and trick it into thinking there is a rig attached. But I'll have to keep a hold of it, or it'll trigger the pod's thruster." Fawn nodded as he spoke, focusing on the mechanics of the problem.

I nodded at him and engaged my thrusters. He followed and we slowly moved to the pod.

"You'll need to hold it long enough for the Inquisitor to exit the pod, then it can fly into a moon for all I care."

We got to the external hatch moments later. Dang was hovering nearby and stayed several feet from the hull.

Fawn slowly and carefully moved to the hatch as the thrusters on the back of the ship silently exploded into white light. I watched a massive hunk of thruster and hull rocketing away from the ship.

Fawn disengaged his thrusters and cautiously took hold of an external handle near a junction box. He pulled out a few tools from a pouch and stuck them to a magnetic cuff and got to work. The hatch opened in short order. Dang and I both flinched. We couldn't hear it, but we knew the hiss and click a hatch like that made inside a ship.

After several moments of no one moving, I released my held breath and heard two answering exhalations. I hadn't been the only one who had been waiting for the blinding white light.

"Captain Hedge." The Inquisitor's voice was loud in the silence.

Fawn jerked and one of his tools flew backwards. Dang caught it and handed it back without comment. He just nodded his thanks and kept working.

"I'd prefer radio silence. We're at the hatch now. Sit tight." I replied.

"Captain Hedge, I do not believe Doctor Finis is on the ship any longer."

"Why do you think that?" I asked the question, but my gut twisted.

I looked again at where the thruster had broken off the ship. The white beam of light that had shorn it off hadn't disappeared. The edges of the hole it had come from were flickering with a slightly dimmer white light. It was getting brighter.

"I believe the Doctor is coming outside to investigate the noises he heard. Might I suggest a faster pace?" The Inquisitor was no longer whispering. The fear in his voice was palpable.

Fawn started shaking as he worked. The titanium nose cap of the pod floated past me as Fawn rooted around in the guts.

"Fawn, we need to move. Now. Noise be damned, just get it

done."

"Working on it." My panic was reflected in his voice.

Dang had her rifle back up, trained on the rear of the ship.

"Hey Hedge!" Jive suddenly shouted over the comms. "I got an idea!"

"What!?"

"Remember that shit above Tarlyn Prime?"

"No!" I was screaming into the channel. "Jive, you hear me? No! *Strix* was in drydock for over a month and we were paying off the repair debt for more than a year. This is no time for antics. We're just about done here." Fawn shook his head as he kept working. I swallowed. "Almost done."

"Captain." Jive had a serious voice on now. "I am detecting an energy signature exiting the rear of the *First Stone* that could power a galactic jump. And it has moved from the center of the ship to the rear in less time than the *Strix* could manage at full burn. You have no time, Hedge."

"We also do not have a second ship! We need the *Strix* whole to get us out of here. How do you think you could pull off the same trick without a second ship!?"

The light had become a pulsing orb like a small sun as it exited the rear of the ship. My UV screen kept flashing darker and darker as I looked at the orb. I couldn't see the other stars in the void. The ship itself was just a dark suggestion of a shape in my peripheral.

But I could see.

Inside the orb, like a charcoal sketch on white paper was the suggestion of a human shape. Arms outstretched, edges fuzzy and fluctuating. The figure disappeared in profile as it turned around. I saw what must have been a face. Still charcoal black but with pinpricks of white showing where the eyes should be. Scared stiff, I was unable to look away.

Then I saw another silhouette. Rocketing directly at the glowing orb was the pale, hairless android. On a direct collision course.

"Jive! No!"

"Yes Hedge. It is the only way. Good luck."

They collided with the orb. The Doctor. In my shocked state I could only watch as Jive rammed into the orb. It sent them both tumbling past the end of the ship and out of my sight.

I was brought back to reality as I felt the pod bump me. It slowly drifted out of the hatch. My UV shade had reduced, and I could see Fawn curled into a tight ball against the exterior of the pod. With one hand gripping an external handle on the pod and the other deep inside a junction box. He was holding off the thruster from firing. His eyes were squeezed shut.

I reached out and got hold of the pod myself. I moved to the hatch at the back. I wanted to tell the kid he did well, but I couldn't summon up any words. First Peeps, now Jive. We lost two crew for this asshole.

Rage ate my sorrow and fear. I yanked the manual release for the hatch. With a puff it flew away to hit the ship. Inside was a tall man in the safety orange of an emergency EVS.

His dark skin and chiseled jaw were bruised. Black rings under his eyes and long, hooked bleeding nose said he had broken it before he was inside his suit. His void-black hair was still wavy and perfect inside the helmet. And those dark golden eyes bore holes through me as he looked at me.

"Nice to meet you, Captain Hedge. Shall we?" He waved a hand behind me. I looked and saw *Strix* pulling up under us. Dang was already floating toward the airlock.

Still holding onto the pod handle, I turned back and punched him right in the visor. "You owe me another android, ya smug fuck."

I heard him growl as we both pushed off the pod towards my ship. Fawn kicked off and the pod suddenly accelerated away as the thruster engaged. The three of us flew towards the airlock.

The Inquisitor caught a hand hold first. I almost missed but Fawn slipped right passed the hatch. I reached for his ankle, but the Inquisitor was faster and had longer arms. He caught Fawn and pulled him back towards the airlock with a jerk.

"Uh… thanks mister." Fawn stammered as he swung into the airlock.

I cut in before anyone else could start talking. "Thanks later, lets get the hell outta here." My UV filter had started to shift again. I looked up and saw the white orb cresting the rear of the wreck. "Fucking go!"

They hadn't needed my urging. We all shoved into the airlock. I was last in and hit the lock. The hatch snapped closed. We all fell hard into a pile on the floor as the gravity kicked in. The Inquisitor was first on his feet and dragged me up with him. I nodded, slammed the interior button, ran the eight meters from airlock to helm and threw myself into the pilot seat.

"Hey Hedge!" Jive's voice greeted me pleasantly as I slipped the goggles over my eyes.

"Jive?!?"

"Yep! I knew you wouldn't survive another cycle without me." They giggled in my ear as I started up the hard-light drive. "I put my central processor in *Strix* for you!"

"We'll talk about this later." I hadn't had the time to think about an AI lose in my ship. "Can you still fly?"

I heard them giggle in answer. Suddenly the ship was turning. The orb-Doctor-thing was in front of us now. My brain panicked and

I tried to punch in a trajectory. The computer didn't respond. It was rotating through directions faster than I could read them. One set stayed on the view and the drive kicked on with the tell-tale whine.

The Orb was glowing brighter in front of us as the drive wound up.

"Jive, now! We NEED to GO!"

I watched as the silhouette at the center of the orb seemed to raise an arm towards the ship. The white light intensified further than my UV filter could keep up with. My eyes felt like they were being burned out. I was screaming in pain when I felt my gut drop behind my spine. It was suddenly black.

The UV filter slowly faded back. Streaking blurs of black and white could be seen on the viewscreen.

We were in jump.

"We made it..." I said. Then leapt out of my seat and threw up noisily in the vac-sink.

The hatch hissed open next to me. Dang was pushing Fawn through. I groped blindly, found my blue shirt from earlier and quickly wiped my mouth as I stood back up.

I nodded to Dang, knowing what she was expecting. I moved over to the crash cot and kicked at the bottom of it. The bulkhead sprang open and I reached down, pulling out an old and dusty bottle of scotch. The label was skewed, faded beyond reading. But I knew my favorite just by looking at it.

"Kid saved our asses, Cap." Dang spoke into the silence as I retrieved three glasses.

"Comin from Dang, that's damn near flirtatious as a complement. Enjoy it's fleeting glory." I grinned at Dang as I poured the scotch. She gave me the finger.

Fawn's pale cheeks burned crimson. "Ah, it was nothin. Jive was the real hero today."

"Thank you Fawn! I shall remember that the next time Hedge lets me order provisions!" Jive's high-pitched voice came over the helm speakers.

I cringed at the tone. "I hope your voice isn't stuck like that. But alright, serious though, this is an debrief. To a... mostly successful haul. And to Peeps, may he rest at peace in the void." As I spoke the words, I flicked some of the scotch at the deck and I heard Dang repeat the words.

Fawn turned to leave. Dang yanked him back by the harness. "Oi! Crew don't leave the debrief less they bleedin!" She scolded, but her tone was friendly.

"I... uh, well last time you had a debrief, you all told me I was a temp and to get out." He said quietly.

"Yeah well, today you saved our asses. Quite literally. Couldn't have done it without ya. I have no idea how to manual release a pod. And unless you can shoot it free, Dang here ain't any better. So, there you have it." I handed him a glass with a finger full of scotch and clinked it with my own. Dang smashed hers into both of ours with a grin. "Welcome to the crew, Fawn. May god or otherwise save your soul."

About the Editor and the Publisher

Stories Rule Press is a family-run micropress in Alberta, Canada, working as a cooperative to bring great story-tellers together and assist them with publication.

Editor Mark Posey is one of the original authors with Stories Rule Press. He edits fiction and non-fiction for various bestselling authors, and for Stories Rule Press. He also writes and publishes his own crime thriller fiction.

Find some of SRP's fiction at *https://StoriesRulePress.com.*

Science Fiction

Thrillers

Fantasy & Urban Fantasy

Romance

www.ingramcontent.com/pod-product-compliance
Lightning Source LLC
Chambersburg PA
CBHW051140020726
47501CB00005B/1604